The Quest for Drisilas

Alice G. Bjornstedt

Table of Contents

Also in the Orlell Chronicles

for Joseph, whose loyalty rivals Glentree's,

Sam, who first discovered the kragons,

and Noah, who remains the inspiration for Mel.

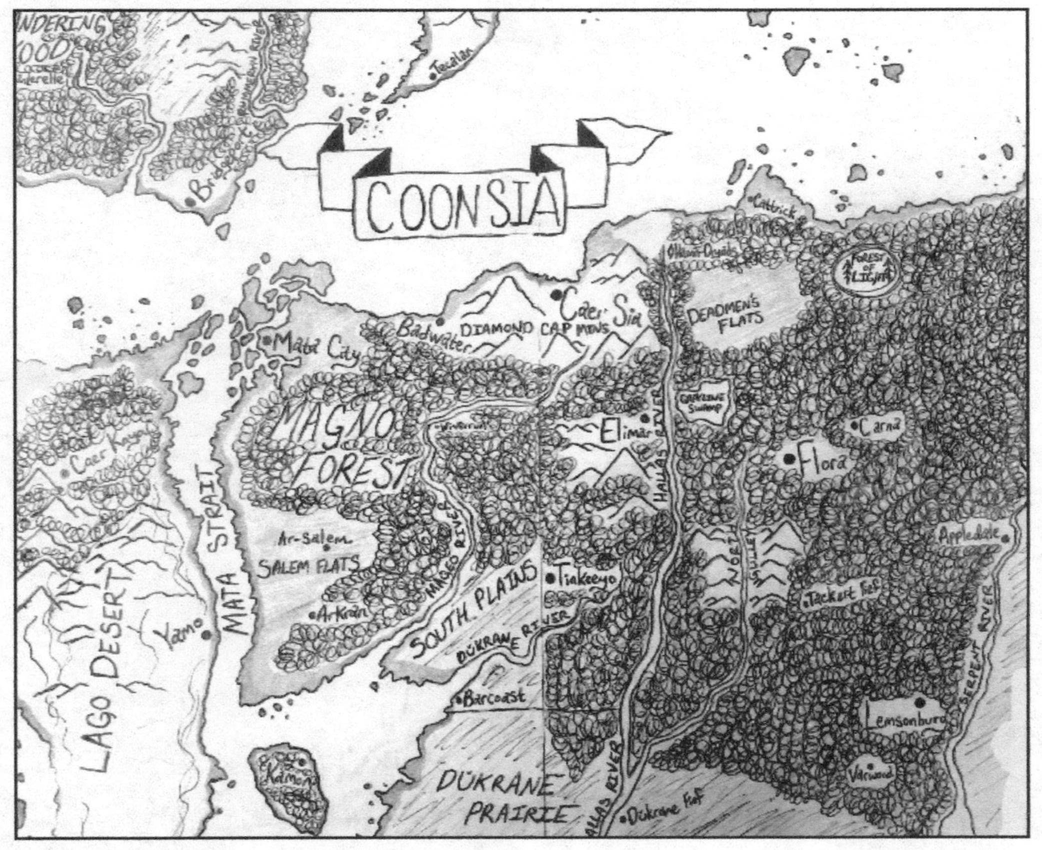

COONSIA
WANDERING WOOD
Interelle
Brd...
RUNNERIN RIVER
Tecalan
Cattrick
Old Mar Druids
FOREST of LIGHT
DEADMEN'S FLATS
Caer Sia
Badwater
DIAMOND CAP MTNS
Mata City
MAGNO FOREST
Caer
LAGO DESERT
Yarro
MATA STRAIT
Ar-Salem
SALEM FLATS
Ar-Kran
Kalmar
Wiverun
Elimar
HALLAS RIVER
Grayleave Swamp
Carna
Flora
NORTH VALLEY
SOUTH PLAINS
MAGEO RIVER
Tiakeeyo
DUKRANE RIVER
Barcoast
Appledale
Tackart For.
SERPENT RIVER
Lemsonburg
Varwood
DUKRANE PRAIRIE
ALLAS RIVER
Dukrane Fork

PART 1

The Sword

Prologue

Early morning in Caer Sia…

In the shadows of the corridor, a deeper darkness lurked. He could feel it, sense the almost palpable cold and evil that clung to it like a shroud. The way it had waited for them all to gather here, in Castle Sia's great halls, blocking the only escape, would prove to be fatal for the inhabitants here. Perhaps the intruding shadow had an intelligence of some kind—perhaps it had concocted this attack in whatever mind it possessed.

The memories swirled in his subconscious mind, fragmented and incomplete. A day he had lived through, years before—except now, he was a bystander, forced to stand and watch, unable to warn the other Liznees. Unable to alter the past.

He saw it sweeping forward, ribbons of black shadow that filled the room, as ice crept up the walls of the room. The Liznee courtier nearest to the door saw it first, and his warning echoed through the hall, breaking the solemn yet hopeful silence that had filled the scene up until now.

And then the black shadows became hateful, a wicked wraith that clouded the room like acrid smoke, choking the nearest bystanders, smothering their screams of pain. Ice shattered the stain glass windows, showering the fleeing Liznees in shards of glass.

He ran, stumbling, panic filling him as he swung his gaze around desperately for his brother and mother, both of whom had vanished into that dark cloud—

"Wake up, sir, there's trouble—"

Voices broke into his mind, overlapping the fading screams of the dream—

Dandio jolted awake.

Faint white light leaked through the thick curtains above the headboard of his bed; morning had barely arrived. His blankets lay in a heap on the floor, indicating that sometime during the night he had flung them off. His wife Ajaha's side of the bed was empty—of course, she had left yesterday to Badwater, where she would meet with the town leaders to discuss the trade routes. She'd be gone for the next few weeks.

The voice beyond the door brought him to his feet. He recognized it as belonging to the captain of guard. From the soldier's tone alone, he guessed there was trouble.

Dandio opened the door, nearly bumping into the speaker, who stood directly beyond it. The captain stepped back, then straightened and saluted hurriedly. "Sir—beg pardon—the watchmen have sounded the alarm. A large creature has been sighted in the hills to the north."

"What sort of creature?" Dandio asked, already buckling on his sword. He trusted the other man's judgment in these matters. The captain wouldn't have woken him in such urgency unless there was trouble.

"A great beast," the captain stammered as they started down the hall, towards the stairs that led up to the castle walls. "They say it looks like a huge dragon, bigger than any native species here. It flew off into the hills a few minutes ago, but it may come back."

"A dragon?" Dandio repeated, half to himself. That didn't seem right. He knew most of the guardsmen personally. Human and Liznee soldiers alike, they all had experience enough to identify a dragon. So the captain was probably right. If it was a dragon, it wasn't native to Coonsia.

"It isn't a dragon," came another voice to their right, as they started up the steps. Ĵan Ki, king of the Liznees of Coonsia, walked towards them, his face serious. "We have reason to believe it is the renegade kragon."

The captain frowned, confused. "A kragon? But they are allied with us, aren't they, sire?"

"Most of them," Dandio told him. They reached the ramparts, a crisp northerly breeze whistling over the stone walls. Caer Sia's red and silver banner fluttered and snapped in the wind above them. Below them, the downtown area of the city stretched on below. To the right, the wild, tangled wilderness of the foothills sprawled on for miles, overshadowed by the purple-gray tips of the mountains that cradled the valley of Sia.

Dandio studied the terrain, thinking. The lingering darkness of the dream seemed to have slowed his thoughts. That, and the early hour, he thought wryly. "Gather your troops," he told the captain. "Stand by on the west wall, and await my orders. I'll be there shortly."

The captain nodded and retreated down the stairs, his chainmail clinking.

"What do you think?" Ĵan asked quietly when the captain left. His green eyes, usually calm, had a light of worry, and there were lines of concern on his silver-skinned face.

Dandio turned to his brother, taking a breath. "If it's a kragon, then it has to be Adderstrike. Unless Lord Fireclaw intends to pick a fight with us."

"No, I trust him well enough. And the report clearly stated that Adderstrike has deserted the Order," Ĵan said. He paused. "Are you all right?"

Dandio looked at him and flashed a tight smile. "Yes, I'm fine. Only thinking."

The echoes from his dream floated through his mind like a draft of cold air—screams, cries, moans from the injured—sad echoes from years before. Chilling with the despair and death that they carried. It made it harder for him to focus on the current issue, and clearly, Ĵan could tell.

A rumbling snarl snapped him out of his thoughts, and they both turned as a winged beast burst from the trees of the woods some hundred yards from the castle walls.

Dandio took an involuntary step back at the shock, and stared at the creature as it approached. Nearly twenty feet long, covered in plated gray scales, its huge wings created a wingspan of nearly thirty feet as it circled the castle. Its head was lean, with a long, ugly muzzle packed with razor sharp teeth that opened in a second snarling scream as it swept toward them.

"Light above," Ĵan murmured.

"Guns! Now!" Dandio shouted, jogging down the wall. Caer Sia's military stood apart from the rest of the Mainland militia with their possession of firearms. Now the cannons, nearly fifty in all, were pulled into position by the guards.

"Wait," Jan said. He followed Dandio, his eyes on the kragon. Adderstrike had circled the walls, and now rose above the castle, his huge wings pounding the air, snarling.

"What's he doing here?" Dandio called back to him, drawing his sword and stepping forward to join his troops. The soldiers, disciplined and battle-ready as they were, had shrank back at the beast's sudden appearance. Such creatures were long forgotten by the common people of Caer Sia, though forever remembered by a few seasoned soldiers who had faced them before.

Jan's eyes met his on the other side of the rampart, and Dandio could see the confusion written on the king's face. And Dandio was just as puzzled. Adderstrike had left the Kragon Order, rebelled against his ruling lord, and now it seemed he planned to attack Caer Sia alone—but why?

"Easy, men," Dandio said to the gunners, who stood, poised and ready to fire if the kragon drew any closer. Still Adderstrike made no attempt to attack, only swept forward and past the walls like an angry falcon, his chest vibrating in that hateful snarl.

Then a weak voice spoke from behind. "Sir..."

Dandio turned sharply. Stumbling up the stairs behind them, bleeding from numerous wounds, was the captain of guard. He caught the injured man as he fell.

"You're all right—hold on—what is it?"

"Below..." the captain choked, his voice rasping. "They... fought their way in… Terrax and his warriors… they're after the sword."

The words sent a jolt through him. Adderstrike was not here to fight; he was a diversion. Which meant he had joined with another group of outlaws…

Outlaws—that had fought their way into the palace.

"Jan, they're below!" he called to his brother, then jogged down the stairs into the palace. The sounds of fighting came from the ground level. He ran, taking the stairs in groups at a time, gripping his sword.

The foyer just within the gates leading out to the courtyard was eerily silent. Bodies lay scattered on the ground, some Liznee soldiers, and others in tattered, filthy clothing. On the wall directly next to the doors, scrawled in charcoal, were written five words.

Terrax will have his throne.

Dandio pushed through the castle doors and jogged out into the courtyard, looking around. A man stood on the far end of the courtyard, long dark hair hanging over his eyes, clutching the sword Drisilas in its scabbard to his chest. Adderstrike dropped down and lifted the outlaw in his claws. Dandio saw the fleeting flash of the outlaw's triumphant smirk before they were gone.

Dandio entered the foyer again, taking a deep breath. His body trembled with the lingering adrenaline and rage. They had been tricked. Drisilas, Jan's sword, had been taken.

Drisilas was no ordinary sword.

Jan appeared on the stairs, with a group of guards behind him. His green eyes took in the scene in a moment, then came to rest on the message on the wall.

"Terrax," Dandio confirmed for him, spitting the name like a curse. "Adderstrike was his ride out. He killed the guards at the gates. That's the reason we weren't alerted." He surveyed the bodies. Three of them stood out from the other intruders—small and stocky, with wiry dark hair and tanned skin. Dwarves, he realized with a jolt of surprise. Members of the Black Dwarve tribe to the east. Had they joined with…?

A tall, thin man approached hesitantly, and Jan looked up. "Well, Drona, what do you make of this?"

His steward and advisor, Pellion Drona, shook his head slowly. "I must admit, sire—I don't know. You say you saw no coat of arms, no sign as to who they served?"

"None," Jan answered him. "Terrax and Adderstrike can't have acted alone—they don't have the power. My guess is they were hired to attack."

"Hired by whom?" Pellion asked uncertainly. A heavy silence settled on the room, leaving the question unanswered.

Dandio glanced outside, in the direction the kragon had gone, and took a breath. "Safacon has fallen—but we knew the peace would not last." He paused. "I will find the sword."

"Dandio…" Jan started uncertainly.

"I'll go after Terrax," Dandio repeated, determination bright in his green eyes. "I'll find Drisilas while you figure out who hired Terrax and his men."

"Then I want to come with you," came a young voice from behind them.

Dandio turned as his daughter, Asescia, approached timidly, her long dark hair still tousled from sleep. Her eyes were wide and fearful as she took in the carnage in the room. But he saw a familiar light of determination in them, too.

"They will have better use of you here," he told her gently as she reached them. "Learning who hired Terrax, determining how to stop him—your uncle will need your help." He grinned faintly at Ĵan, who only nodded and laid a hand on Asescia's shoulder.

"Stay," he said gently as the teenage Liznee girl hesitated. "Pellion and I will appreciate your help and perspective."

Asescia nodded slowly. Dandio hugged her tightly, feeling a familiar stab at regret of leaving her. It could—and probably would—be a long time before he saw her again.

All the same, he almost looked forward to the approaching hunt. The time had come to stop Adderstrike and the arrogant Terrax.

"Send for Glentree, and Captain Tarash," he told Drona, who nodded and jogged off. He placed his hands on Asescia's shoulders, meeting her eyes. "Help your uncle learn who hired them, and what the Kragon Order is up to. And be safe."

"I will," Asescia said. She straightened, then turned to follow Pellion Drona.

Dandio looked at Ĵan and clasped the king's hand. "It'll be good to get back out there. Don't worry about me. I will deal with Terrax."

"And…what of the Darkness?" his brother asked quietly.

Dandio paused. A chill ran down his spine as he remembered the report that had come only yesterday…a report that spoke of ancient evil reawakened in the heart of the country. An evil forgotten for decades, now stirring again.

For an instant his hand strayed to the scar creasing his face, and his determination faltered as the old nightmare flooded his head.

Then he looked up and nodded shortly. "I will find the sword. But I'll have help."

1

The Gift

Three weeks later. In Appledale, Daffodalion…

"Happy birthday, Mel. Feel old yet?"

A book on his plump belly, Mr. Joseph Smallbutton studied his son, his eyes twinkling teasingly. Like many fathers, he fancied himself a highly amusing person and wasn't concerned by the fact that no one else thought the same.

Mel had paused by the table and looked wearily at his father. As is common with many pre-teenage boys, he found nothing funny in his father's unoriginal jokes. "Yep, a whole year, Dad," he said, playing along. "Pretty soon I'll be old and gray."

"That'd be unfortunate—haven't seen many old and gray eleven-year-olds." His father chuckled at his own wit, then went back to his book.

Mel looked out the window. The sun streamed down upon the cluster of thatch-roof houses that made up their neighborhood. Further down the road, he could see the village, which already bustled with shoppers. A weekend market had been set up along the road. His mother would be out already, purchasing last-minute birthday presents. The thought made his stomach tingle with excitement.

Appledale, a small village several miles east of the larger city of

Flora, Daffodalion, was a peaceful town, positioned between the tangled forests to the west, and the sprawling prairies to the east. Mel could remember, in a sturdy little farmhouse just off the main road. The town itself consisted of a post office and a few shops. On a clear day like this, Mel could see the wide prairie lands stretching on past the township, the green-blue grass contrasting the tawny orange of the autumn leaves.

Mr. Smallbutton put down his book and eyed his son cryptically. "So—Melenburr," he began, using his son's full name in mock seriousness, "what do you want for your birthday?"

Mel thought a moment, running a hand through his tousled red hair. "A sword, maybe," he said after a moment.

He didn't need to think about his answer to that question. He had asked for, dreamed about a sword every year since he'd turned seven, which was the year a garrison of town guard had performed a special program in honor of Appledale's fiftieth birthday. The flashing blades and polished armor had captivated him ever since.

Mr. Smallbutton considered this for a moment. "Maybe," was all he said. Swords were not exactly something one came across in an everyday market. Besides, Mel knew, they were expensive. His family had enough to put food on the table each night, but not much else. But he allowed himself to hope otherwise. Snow had not yet blocked the northern mountain passes, and the merchants and peddlers would make their way to the prairie villages in one last trip before the winter. Maybe one of those merchants would sell swords, and maybe—just maybe—he'd sell them cheap.

The door opened, and Mrs. Smallbutton entered, carrying several baskets. Unlike her burly husband, she was slightly built and petite, with wispy blonde hair and hazel eyes. "Good morning—happy birthday, Mel—help me put this on the table, will you, Joseph?"

Mel's father stood and lifted the baskets, carrying them into the kitchen. Mel watched carefully, hoping to get a peek at one of his gifts. He was nearly knocked over as a small figure tackled him from behind.

"Happy birthday! I got you something!"

Mel detached himself from the determined grip, grinning. His little sister Misty, who was seven, beamed up at him, holding her arms behind her back. Now she triumphantly produced what she held, which was a slightly squashed piece of candy wrapped in shiny paper.

"Thanks, Misty," Mel said, pocketing the candy. "I'll eat it after breakfast," he added, as Misty frowned. This seemed to satisfy her.

Their parents were talking in the kitchen, and Mel could only catch bits and pieces of their conversation. But their tones surprised him; his mother sounded excited, and his father stunned.

"I don't know where it came from either, Joseph—but isn't it lovely? Look at the stone in the hilt…"

"Good gracious, Elonie—I can't believe—do you know how much these are…"

"Of course—but I got it for three shekels, only three—it's exactly what he's been wanting…"

They both stopped talking as Mel and Misty entered the kitchen. Mel looked at them curiously. "What is it?"

His mother had subtly hid something behind her back, and

smiled quickly. "Top secret birthday things. Don't you worry."

Mel started to protest, but realized he would probably get no more information out of either of them until after lunch.

The day went exactly as he had been hoping. Breakfast of sausages and eggs was followed by a long afternoon of playing with his friends outside in the early autumn sun. Then, finally, they all traipsed back inside and settled down in the parlor before supper for his presents. His friends watched enthusiastically over his shoulder as he opened his gifts, each one wrapped neatly in burlap and ribbon by his mother.

"One more," Misty told him, her face lit with excitement as her brother looked up expectantly.

Elonie Smallbutton appeared from the hall, holding something behind her back. "All right now, I didn't wrap this one, Mel. So hold out your hands and close your eyes."

Mel obeyed and reached out. He heard a rustle as his mother approached…then a collective gasp from his small audience. Something long and heavy rested in his hands.

"Open your eyes, Mel."

Mel opened his eyes and stared. In his hands he held a sheathed sword, the scabbard protected in tattered rags. The hilt above it was made of tarnished steel, and a single blue stone was set there.

"Mom, how did you…" Mel stammered in awe, at a loss for words. He ran his hands down the scabbard, the rough cloth against his hands reassuring him that the beautiful blade he held was real.

"Draw it, son," his father encouraged from his chair by the fireplace.

Mel's hand closed eagerly on the hilt, and he pulled. The sword… didn't budge. He frowned and tugged again with the same result. A few of his friends giggled, and he felt himself flush.

"Must be stuck," Joseph Smallbutton told his son, stepping over and taking the hilt. He gave a mighty heave, intending to whip the sword free in a very heroic action.

The blade remained where it was. The sword was stuck solidly in the weathered scabbard.

Several of his friends took turns tugging at the sword, trying to dislodge it. Their results were the same as Mel's own. Mel looked dismally at the sword, peering at the place where the blade rested inside the scabbard. There was no rust, no sign of something that had stuck the sword there. The sword sat firmly—even stubbornly—in its place.

"Perhaps that's why it was so cheap, Elonie," Mel's father chuckled, taking the sword and studying it carefully. "Oddest thing. It doesn't look like there's a thing wrong."

"There's nothing wrong with it," Mel said, a little defensive of his gift. "It…just doesn't want to come out."

Joseph raised his eyebrows. "I'll agree with that, son—I only meant there doesn't seem to be anything stopping it from coming out." He eyed the scabbard again, then shrugged. "Well, no matter. In the morning I'll take it over to the blacksmith's. They'll be able to get it out."

"Never mind the blacksmiths; I'd like to speak with Mr. Bandle," Elonie decided. "He organizes the weekly market. I'd like to know if we were sold a broken sword, and if so he could contact the peddler." She looked at

Joseph, then back at her son. "How about you stay and watch Misty, and we'll go talk to Mr. Bandle?"

Mel nodded, still disappointed. His mother was clearly determined, which made him feel a little better.

His friends returned to their homes just before supper. Their parents left just after that, with Elonie still muttering about cheating peddlers and bad merchandise.

This left Mel in charge. Misty wanted to play chess, and lead the way outside in the cool of early evening carrying the board and sack of pieces. Mel followed, wearing the sword over his shoulders. Even if he couldn't draw it, he still enjoyed the weight and feel of the weapon.

"Where did you and Mom find this?" he asked her as they settled down in the grass.

"Market," Misty said importantly. "There was a peddler there we haven't seen before."

"Oh?" Mel asked, setting up the chess pieces. That was odd, he thought distractedly. They didn't often get new peddlers coming through town, except in the summer time or during winter holidays. At this time of year, the only sellers at market would be either locals, or the occasional spice merchant. Either way, Appledale rarely saw any peddlers selling items as valuable as a sword like this.

He fingered the scabbard, hands running over the tattered cloth. His fingers snagged on a loose bit of fabric, pulling it down slightly and exposing a gleam of leather from beneath. Mel frowned at it, startled. "Misty, look...I don't think this is the real scabbard."

His sister scooted close to him as Mel pulled away the pieces of cloth. His hands came away stained gray and sticky—the rags had been stuck to the scabbard with some sort of glue. Mel's heart was suddenly pounding in excitement.

The last strip of cloth came away in Mel's hand, and he stared in awe at the true scabbard. Made of polished black leather, with silver thread running along the edges, it molded perfectly around the blade within. Mel's eyes were drawn to a silver symbol embroidered at the opening—an X, with a line on the top of it and a second line below, like an hourglass with the bottom falling out.

"That's the Liznee symbol," Misty informed him unexpectedly.

Mel looked at her. "Really?"

"Yes—I learned about emblems at school. That's the emblem of Caer Sia."

"Caer Sia?" Mel repeated, surprised. Caer Sia was the capital of the neighboring country of Coonsia, miles and miles from here. If this sword was truly a Liznee blade, then how had it got here? Besides that… why had the sword been disguised?

A drop of rain hit Mel on the nose, and he looked up. Daylight was fading fast, and an overcast of clouds covered the sky. "Come on, Misty. It's getting dark and it's raining. I'll ask Dad about the sword when he gets back tonight. Maybe he'll know something about it."

Despite the temptation to stay up late with his parents gone, Mel knew his mother wanted them both in bed on time. He tucked Misty in. She already looked sleepy, but equally curious. "Maybe the peddler stole it," she suggested sleepily as Mel left her room. "Maybe he fought a Liznee and stole his sword."

"Maybe. Night," Mel agreed, and walked down the short hall to his bedroom. Misty was smart for her age, and Mel knew she would be as eager to solve this mystery as he was. But right now, he needed to be alone with his own thoughts for a little while.

So he sat on the foot of his bed, the open window letting in breaths of chill evening air and the sound of the sprinkling rain, and studied the sword. He fingered the emblem at the edge of the scabbard—the emblem of Caer Sia, if Misty was right…

What was it doing here? Maybe the peddler had bought the sword in Caer Sia, and then come here to sell it? But then, why disguise the scabbard, especially since the sword's true beauty would fetch a higher price than what his mother would have gotten it for?

Unless, of course, the peddler's main goal had been to get rid of the sword quickly, and not focus on the profit…

"Maybe it was stolen," Mel murmured to himself. That was the only answer that accounted for both the sword's disguise and its affordable price. His mother would hopefully get answers from Mr. Bandle, he thought. They would be back soon.

Another thought occurred to him, suddenly. If the sword had been stolen from Caer Sia, what if its rightful owner came looking for it?

Then, from down the hall, he heard Misty scream.

2

The Rider

Mel jumped to his feet at his sister's shrill cry. Misty had nightmares every few nights or so, products of her overactive imagination. But she hadn't been asleep long enough for that.

"Misty!" he called, worry gnawing at the pit of his stomach as he jogged down the short hall to her room. He flung open her door—and stopped in his tracks.

Misty was sitting up in bed, tangled in her blankets, shrinking away from the open window directly across from the door. Something huge hunched in the window frame, already halfway inside the room. Mel turned up the oil lamp, allowing the wick to burn brighter, and his stomach lurched as the light fell on the hideous creature before them.

Mud-red scales plated the creature's body, a long, slithering form that made it hard to tell where body became tail. Its shoulders rose in two bat-like wings, which were now wedged partway into the room. The creature's face was triangular, with large, bulbous white eyes. It let out a low, ominous hiss, revealing rows and rows of teeth. Its front fangs looked nearly three inches long.

Misty screamed again and thrashed her way out of the bed, falling to the floor. Her piercing scream seemed to aggravate the monster; it flinched back slightly, then hissed again, and crept the rest of the

28

way down the wall into the room before drawing itself upright. Its head was level with Mel's, and its coiling body would have spanned the length of the room.

"Mama!" Misty cried, sobbing with fear as she scrambled away from the winged snake. Mel had frozen in shock, his body trembling from terror as the snake's eyes locked on his. Then, seeming to vibrate out of the creature's chest, came a hollow, echoing voice.

"Drisilas."

Mel grabbed Misty's hand, pulling her behind him as they edged out of the room. "W-what?" he managed to stammer.

The white eyes stopped him in his tracks—the way the creature studied them chilled Mel to his very core. Not like they were scared, confused children. Nor as if they were enemies to be trifled with. The look in those emotionless white eyes told Mel that they were targets, completely helpless. Prey.

"*Drisilas,*" the creature rasped again. "*The Dark One requires the stone of Drisilas. Terrax must not have it.*"

"We—who's—we're not Terrax," Mel said shakily, holding Misty's hand in his, and clutching the sword to his chest with his other hand. The sword! Suddenly, he understood. This creature had come for the sword—this strange, mysterious sword that had shown up out of nowhere—

He pushed Misty out of the room, into the hall, then grabbed the door and slammed it closed in the creature's face. "Come on!" he said, grabbing Misty's hand, and they ran into the parlor.

"What is that thing?" Misty choked through her tears.

"I don't know—we'll be okay, come on, let's go to the neighbor's," Mel gasped. His mind reeled in confusion and panic. What was going on? Where had the creature come from?

They had nearly reached the front door when a horrible scraping sound reached their ears. They stumbled back just in time as the monster smashed through the front door, its powerful wings gouging two gashes in the wood, that shuddering rasping hiss sending chills down Mel's spine. He and Misty raced into the kitchen and dropped down under the table.

From the parlor, the echoing voice spoke, repeating the same word. *"Drisilas,"* it hissed, over and over again. The soft sound of scales against the hardwood floor grew louder as the creature crept toward the kitchen. *"Drisilas. Drisilas. Drisilas."*

Misty whimpered—Mel pulled her close, covering her mouth with his hand, his heart pounding.

Then, from the other room, the creature's voice grew low as the words changed. *"Prey. Find. Kill."*

Mel was shaking so hard he was sure his teeth would start chattering. Cold sweat ran down his face. The sliding sound drew closer, and the creature entered the kitchen, still hissing the mantra of the three words. *"Prey. Find. Kill."*

"Mel…" Misty whispered. Terrified tears ran down her cheeks. The creature's face appeared as it peered at them under the table. Its forked tongue lashed inches from their faces, taking in their scents in triumph.

They both screamed. Mel pushed Misty away, towards the front door—he grabbed the sheathed sword and swung it at the creature's head. The hilt made contact with the monster's neck, and it jerked back with a furious hiss. Mel scrambled out from under the table and ran for the door.

Something grabbed him from behind, pinning him flat on his back. The creature hissed, sending droplets of saliva down on his face as it bared its huge fangs. Mel screamed and struggled, trying to push the creature off, but to no avail. Outside, Misty's cries were nearly drowned out in the pouring rain. Someone had to hear— someone had to hear them and come help—

Someone did.

Through the open door, Mel saw a figure cross the road and reach him just in time to slash across the creature's face. The stranger's sword was illuminated in a brilliant flicker of lightning as he struck again, forcing the snake off of Mel. His cloak billowed as he moved, the hood shading his face. The snake snarled, then lunged, snapping at him, and the stranger cut at its shoulder again. The creature recoiled, snarling— Mel saw the flash of white teeth as the stranger grinned.

"On your feet—go down the road," the man ordered. Mel obeyed, absolutely at a loss as to what was happening, but in no position to argue. He saw the swordsman strike again, and now the snake fled, barely escaping the stranger's strike as it took flight.

The stranger's face set in displeasure as he watched the creature flee, but he turned away and jogged after the siblings. They ran down the road toward the township.

The stranger motioned for them to stop; he raised his fingers to his mouth and blew a shrill whistle. A large animal bounded out of the shadowed woods to their left, nearly the size of a pony, but with a feline grace and strong, lean limbs. It let out a hoarse cry in response to the whistle. Shaggy fur covered its body, and its feathered wings were poised for flight as it stopped in front of them.

"A gryphon," Mel managed to choke, still in shock.

"Nice job, you identified at least one beast tonight—now up you go," their rescuer ordered. He sheathed his sword and lifted them up one after the other.

"Where—where are you taking us?" Mel panted, regaining his thoughts.

"I'll tell you in a minute. We have to hurry, there might be more of them on the way," the swordsman said, swinging up in front of them. He clipped his heels against the gryphon's sides, and the beast sprang forward, took several bounds, then spread its wings and lifted into the sky.

Mel clutched frantically at the man's shirt as the ground dropped away beneath them. Rain pelted his face as they surged into the sky. He realized vaguely that they were headed southwest—away from home.

The man looked down, then let out a breath. "All right…I think you're safe now."

Considering they were about a quarter mile in the air, Mel didn't consider that *safe*, but since the man had just saved both their lives, he decided not to mention that. "Who are you?" he managed to pant, looking up curiously at their rescuer.

The man glanced over his shoulder and gave them a crooked

smile. He was younger than Mel had thought at first, maybe in his early twenties, with dark hair cut to shoulder length and a small beard shading his face. There was something roguish and vaguely familiar about him.

"I was about to ask you two the same thing," the stranger said.

"I—I'm—my name's Melenburr—but everyone calls me Mel, because that's shorter and a lot of people misspell Melenburr, and besides I don't like being called Melenburr, so I go by Mel." That sounded complicated even to him, and the stranger frowned slightly. Mel flushed. "I'm Mel, and this is my sister Misty." Misty, who was clutching nervously to Mel's back, managed a shaky smile.

The man smiled back. "Well, it's good to meet you, both of you. As for your first question, I'm taking you back to the camp at present—my companions and I will help sort things out in the morning. But I think I can promise that you're safe from any more serpentines now."

Mel relaxed slightly. There was an easy-going, likable air about the stranger that he trusted.

Misty looked at him curiously. "But who are you?" she asked.

Without turning, the man replied calmly, though his answer sent a shock of surprise through Mel, "My name is Rygal, son of Maran, of Gayrile."

3

The Camp

Rygal. The name was one Mel had only heard spoken in stories around the campfire on summer nights, stories brought home by his father from trips to the border. The stories told of quests and battles, of the fall of the maddened alchemist Kado and, only two years before, of the destruction of Kado's master Safacon. His father had told him those stories—tales of bravery and heroism and chivalry, tales that had enraptured Mel's mind.

For a moment, he was dumbfounded.

"I've heard of you!" he finally blurted. "You—you helped rally the Guardians of Gayrile—you fought alongside them against Safacon! I thought you'd be bigger," he added, then realized how rude that sounded. "No, not bigger—older, I guess—I'd always pictured Rygal of Gayrile to be—a giant, with huge arms and a huge sword and… and…" he trailed off, embarrassed.

The stranger considered this. "Well—sorry for disappointing you. You sound like Glentree, always telling me to grow out, not up."

"No—I don't think you—that's not what I meant," Mel stammered. "I wasn't trying to be offensive," he said instead, flushing deeply.

"Well, it's a good thing I rarely take offense," Rygal said cheerfully. "Now. Less talk about me, I want to know more about you two. And in particular, about where you got that sword." He nodded at the sword, which Mel still held tightly.

Mel's fingers had practically frozen around the scabbard and were numb with the cold, so he had nearly forgotten about it. Now his grasp tightened even more, and he instinctively drew it closer. "I—my mom got it for me for my birthday—I don't think she knew what it was," he stammered, hoping he wouldn't get his whole family in trouble for possessing such a weapon.

Thankfully Rygal nodded. "I don't think so either—don't worry. It's a relief to see that you have it, to put it lightly. Your mother got it at the market, you said?"

"I think so, I don't know—Misty was with her." Mel looked at his sister, who was shivering both from cold and from fear of the encounter.

"You were?" Rygal asked her hopefully. "Where did you get it?"

"I—we didn't know—we thought it was just a sword," Misty said timidly.

"It's all right," Rygal said in a softer tone. "But this particular sword was stolen from Caer Sia a few weeks ago, and we've been trying to get it back… and away from the wrong hands."

"Caer Sia?" Mel repeated. He'd assumed as much by this point, but hearing it out in the open was still stunning.

Rygal looked back at him, his gray-blue eyes penetrating into Mel's. "That sword is Drisilas, the sword of the High King Ĵan Ki. Only he can draw the blade, as its rightful owner."

"This is the High King's sword?" Mel said in surprise. He studied the hilt, and the truth finally dawned on him. He had only heard stories of the great sword Drisilas, but he remembered that the sword was useless to anyone but the High King himself. "So—there wasn't anything wrong with it—that's why I couldn't pull it out."

"Indeed," Rygal said, nodding. "That sword—the stone in its hilt, anyway—was a gift to the High King from the hama-dryads long ago. In short, they made it so that only Jan can draw and wield the blade." He looked at the sword thoughtfully. "But now, there are others who are trying to take it."

Mel looked at him in confusion. "What do you mean?"

"We'll get to that," Rygal said, and glanced back at them. "Misty, what did the man who sold the sword look like?"

Misty's brow furrowed as she thought. "Well…he…he was tall," she offered finally. "He had a scruffy beard and he used bad words—but he sold us the sword for really cheap," she added. "That's the only reason Mama wanted to buy from him."

"I think he wanted to get rid of the sword fast," Mel said. He remembered his earlier theory, and felt quite proud to realize he had come so close to the truth. "Do you think someone stole the sword, realized they couldn't draw it, and then got rid of it fast to throw you off its trail?"

"That's my guess," Rygal said, nodding. He thought a moment. "I'm sorry you two had to get tangled up in this mess."

"You saved us," Misty said, her teeth chattering, as she looked admiringly at Rygal. "From that—that bat-snake thing."

"Why was it after us?" Mel asked, still not understanding that part. "And why did it want the sword?"

"I'm not sure," Rygal said. "That creature was a serpentine, and most likely a servant of someone who wants the sword too."

"A servant?" Mel was surprised.

Rygal nodded. "Serpentines are clever, but with simple, animal minds. However, someone can easily access control to their thoughts—some call it hypnosis, I think. I'm not entirely sure how that works. Either way, serpentines can be controlled to hunt down prey for their master."

"It spoke to us," Mel said. "It…it said it was trying to keep the sword away from someone called Terrax."

Rygal's brow wrinkled. "*Keep* it from Terrax?" he repeated.

"I don't know, it said the Dark One wanted the… the stone of Drisilas," Mel said haltingly. "Who's Terrax?"

Rygal's face was a mix of surprise… and confusion. "The Dark One," he murmured, half to himself. "I'll have to ask about that." He looked back at them, face calm again. "Don't worry about it for now. We're here—hold tight."

The gryphon tucked in her wings and dropped gracefully into the trees. Once on the ground, the forest sheltered them from the wind and rain, and Mel started to feel warmer. He and Misty looked around curiously. A tent had been set up in the shelter of the trees. A shaggy pack pony was tethered nearby. A fire, sheltered by an iron cover, blazed in the center of the camp, sending irregular patterns of light around the woods.

Rygal dismounted and helped both of them do the same. Mel's legs felt stiff and numb after the long, cold flight. Nothing looked familiar to him in the dense wood—they were miles from Appledale by this point. "Where are we?" he asked uneasily.

"Until we can confirm that there are no more serpentines near your town, it's safer for you both to stay here," Rygal explained.

"Don't worry. We'll sort everything out in the morning."

This made sense to Mel. The serpentines could still be patrolling the roads near their house—if he and Misty returned, his parents might be in danger. Misty slipped her cold little hand into his; her eyes were wide and nervous.

A tall, burly figure had appeared out of the shadows. Mel instinctively pulled Misty closer to him as the hulking man approached. The newcomer stood a full head taller than Rygal, and his shoulders were wider than Misty was tall. "Good to see ya back, boy," he said, clapping Rygal on the shoulder. His voice was deep, with a broad accent. "Any luck?"

"Better than luck," Rygal said with a grin. "Look who found the sword." He nodded to the siblings, who stood uncertainly behind him.

The big man's eyes rested on them, and he grinned widely. "Ah, look at that! And who might you two be?"

"I'm—Mel Smallbutton. This is my sister Misty," Mel said quickly, still in awe. The giant dropped to a knee to face them and shook both their hands in turn. Mel's knuckles protested as his hand was gripped in that muscular grasp. Thankfully the big man seemed to notice, and gave Misty's hand a gentler treatment.

"Well now, it's an absolute relief to see you found the sword," the man continued, and saluted in greeting. "Deputy Glentree at yer service, and now in your debt. We've been looking for that for weeks."

He took the sword from Mel's offered hands. The relief and satisfaction on his face surprised Mel. Somehow, he was beginning to guess that there was more about that sword than he had first assumed.

"You finished scouting the Appledale village, then?" Glentree asked Rygal.

"I didn't finish my patrol—had to get these two out of danger. They were trying to convince a serpentine that they didn't much care to be his dinner when I found them," Rygal said.

Glentree raised his bushy eyebrows. "A serpentine?" he repeated.

"A big one," Rygal said grimly. He paused, looking curiously at the older man. "I don't think it served Terrax—besides, from what Llyrion's reported, Terrax hasn't mastered the ability to control them, right?"

"At least as far as we know," Glentree murmured. His brow furrowed in thought as he shook his head. "Well, we'll sort it out in the morn. These two look done out."

"Where's Dandio?" Rygal asked Glentree.

"Tracking. Llyrion saw signs of a Dwarve encampment not too far from here, so they've gone to check."

The unfamiliar words and confusing conversation was starting to overwhelm Mel, but his mind had hinged on one name that Rygal had said. "Dandio?" he repeated slowly. "You mean… Dandio Ki?"

Glentree grinned widely. "The very same, lad, and no better man to lead this venture in these times either, I'd say."

"*The* Dandio Ki?" Mel repeated, stunned.

Rygal nodded. "He'll be back soon. I take it you've heard of him."

Misty piped up before Mel could stop her. "Dandio is Mel's hero. When he was little, he would tie a bed sheet around his neck and fight with a wooden sword and pretend to be Dandio. I was always the princess he rescued. One time—"

"Misty!" Mel interrupted her quickly, feeling his face redden. His embarrassment was forestalled by another question. "Wait, what venture?"

Glentree and Rygal looked like they were both hiding smiles, then Rygal answered. "We'll tell you more in the morning. You both look exhausted."

He led them toward the tent. It sheltered a few packs of gear and was a little tight, but it was warm and dry. After the adrenaline of the last few hours, Mel felt exhausted. But he didn't want to go to sleep just yet, not with so many unanswered questions.

Rygal moved the gear to make space to set up two bedrolls and blankets. He also offered dry tunics, which were a little big but were better than sleeping in wet clothes. "Rest up. I'll explain everything in the morning," he said as he slipped back out into the rain.

Misty settled down under her blankets and yawned. "Mel… what about Mom and Dad? They're going to be really worried about us."

Mel sat on the mat, not sure what to say. He was thinking the very same thing. If Rygal was right, and creatures were patrolling the streets of Appledale looking for two children with a sword, would that place his parents in danger? Either way, they would arrive home to find the house trashed, and no sign of either Mel nor Misty. The thought of his parents calling for them, searching, worrying, sent a stab of pain through Mel's heart.

"It'll be all right," he told her lamely. "Just… try to sleep."

Misty lay awake for a few more minutes, then finally drifted off. Mel could hear her murmuring anxiously in her sleep, most likely dreaming of the chilling serpentine encounter.

He lay in silence for a long while, thinking through the unexpected twist his birthday had taken. He and Misty had, quite suddenly, been thrust into an epic struggle for the sword, and he had no idea what would happen next.

Finally, as the low voices outside faded away and the light from the fire died down, he dozed off.

4

The Hunters

When Mel awoke the next morning, it took him a moment to remember where he was. Then everything came back to him in a flash. The sword for his birthday. The serpentine attacking them. Rygal coming to their rescue, then flying to a camp in the wilderness on the back of a gryphon—

Mel sat bolt upright. "We have to go home!" He untangled himself from the blanket and looked around the little tent. Misty was still asleep. Set aside and neatly folded were their dry clothes. Mel changed quickly, pulled on his shoes, and then gently shook his sister awake.

"Misty, wake up. Time to go home."

Misty looked around owlishly, disoriented for a moment. "Where's Mom?" she asked sleepily.

"We're going to go see her. Come on," Mel said encouragingly, pushing the folded clothes into her hands. "I'll be back—get dressed."

He slipped out through the tent flaps and paused. The rain had stopped, and now the morning light shone through a veil of fog. A second tent was set up to his left, just inside the tree line. Two mats lay under the stooping boughs of the hemlock trees, sheltered from last night's rain. He saw no sign of Rygal or Glentree, but the fire had recently been stoked.

"Good morning."

Mel jumped at the voice behind him and turned quickly. A man walked out of the trees, a bow slung over one shoulder. He carried two skinned rabbits.

"Sorry for startling you," the newcomer added as he entered the camp. Now that he stood in the light, Mel could see him better. He was an Elf, tall and lean, though a little shorter than Rygal. His hair was red-blond, pulled back. His eyes were dark blue, bright and intelligent, set in a face that smiled now. "You are from Appledale? Rygal mentioned you had an unpleasant encounter with a serpentine."

"Yeah, it tried to eat us," Mel said, recovering from his surprise. "I'm Mel," he added quickly.

"Well, good morning, Mel. My name is Llyrion Tarash, captain of Caer Sia." The Elven warrior crossed to the fire, setting the two rabbit carcasses on a simple black pan and slicing the meat into thin strips. He rinsed off his hands, then opened another pack and continued preparing the morning meal. Mel stepped closer to the fire. The warmth was comforting in the chilly morning. Llyrion's name was familiar, and it took him a little while to place it.

"You went on the quest to stop the Hazes," he stated finally, as it occurred to him. "Kado and his Haze army—ten years ago."

"Yes, I did," Llyrion said with another smile. "I take it you've heard a little about that, then."

"Just a little. I always wanted to be a hero and fight warlords," Mel said, then blushed at the childishness of the statement. But Llyrion nodded.

"So did Rygal. So does my son, Alder, as much as it distresses his mother." A light of amusement showed in his eyes as he said it. "Where did you find the sword?"

"It was my birthday gift—my mom bought it at market," Mel said. He looked at the Elf curiously. "Rygal said the sword was stolen—why would it end up at our market?"

"I am not entirely sure, but I believe we shall discuss them after breakfast," Llyrion said. He nodded at a wooden container a few feet away. "Hand me that, could you?"

Mel fetched the wooden jar, which contained a blend of savory spices. Llyrion set a second pan beside the first, and set several slices of bread to toast next to the seasoned rabbit. The smell of cooking meat made Mel's stomach rumble. The excitement from yesterday left him practically famished.

Misty appeared from the tent, blinking sleepily in the sunshine. "Something smells good," she announced, walking over to the fire.

There was a rustle of underbrush, and Glentree walked out of the trees, his ruddy face shining with perspiration. "Mornin', Llyrion, Mel, Misty," he greeted them in turn. He blew out a breath and wiped his brow with the back of his hand. "Is breakfast ready?"

"Should be in a few more moments," Llyrion answered him. "Where's Dandio and Rygal?"

"Rygal wanted to race—he thought his way was the faster way back to camp. Took a 'shortcut', as he calls it, up the hill, even though following the creek is faster," Glentree explained. He looked quite pleased with himself. "I think Dandio's with him, which means I've beaten both of their behinds back to camp."

More rustling came from the trees behind them as Glentree finished speaking. Mel turned in time to see a tall Liznee jog out of the woods. He was out of breath as he looked at Glentree. "Rygal here?"

"Nope," Glentree answered him.

A wide grin of triumph crossed the Liznee's face, making his green eyes twinkle. "Good," he said, and caught his breath before walking over stiffly.

Mel to studied his childhood hero in fascination. Dandio, he saw, stood taller than Llyrion but not as tall as Glentree, and wore a jerkin of plated dark leather over a soft long-sleeve shirt and canvas pants. His boots were travel-worn, indicating many other journeys that he had embarked on. Simple clothes, not the garb Mel had expected of such a legend—all the same, he was in awe to see him.

Dandio noticed Mel and Misty, and smiled to them as he approached. "I take it these are our newest arrivals."

Glentree nodded. "Mel and Misty Smallbutton, of Appledale. Rygal brought them last night."

Dandio extended a hand. His voice was clear, with the distinct elegant Caer Sia accent. "It is good to meet you both," he said. Mel shook his hand, still in awe to be meeting such a person. Dandio had silver-toned skin and chiseled features, much like other Liznees. His ears were slightly pointed, and he had no hair or beard. His eyes were green, and there was a keen and calculating look in them that made Mel think he would be a dangerous opponent. But at the moment, his face was calm and kind. A dark scar ran down the right side of his face, over the eye and down to the jaw.

"I owe both of you my thanks," Dandio was saying, drawing Mel out of his revelry, "for recovering Drisilas. We have been tracking the thieves for several weeks now, and I admit I was beginning to give up hope."

"We got it for Mel's birthday," Misty said. She looked a little put out that these strangers planned on taking her brother's prized birthday present.

"Ah. Well, I apologize for taking it. But perhaps in Sia we can get you a sword that you can actually wield." There was a glimmer of amusement in Dandio's eyes.

Mel finally found his voice. "Oh—no, that's fine, we're glad to help." He was interrupted by Rygal, who jogged into camp. The young warrior put his hands on his knees to catch his breath for a moment, then straightened. His face fell as he saw both Glentree and Dandio standing there.

"You beat me back?" Rygal panted incredulously.

"Substantially," Dandio informed him with a barely concealed grin.

"I beat you both," Glentree said loudly, beaming. "Told ya to follow the creek. It saves the walk up out of the gully."

Rygal shook his head good-naturedly and sat down by the fire. "What's for breakfast?" he asked Llyrion, who was listening with an amused smile as he turned the slices of bacon.

"Toast and rabbit—it'll be ready in a minute." Llyrion looked at Dandio. "We have bacon and cornmeal left over, so we can have that for noon meal. But we're a little low on food—we'll have to stop for supplies somewhere soon."

"We have bacon," Rygal stated in satisfaction, as though bacon was enough to sustain them.

Dandio nodded to Llyrion. "Very well. It may be worth heading into a small town to pick up more supplies before we head west again." He turned to study the two siblings. "I am curious to hear more about the serpentine that attacked you. You said it spoke?"

"Yes… sir," Mel replied, not sure how to address the Liznee warrior.

Dandio shook his head quickly. "Don't worry about the *sir* part; I was never one for protocol. Just Dandio will do." A half smile crossed his face before he became serious again. "Tell me more about the serpentine."

"Well, it came right after we went to bed," Mel said, glad to offer helpful information. "It said it had come for the sword."

Llyrion looked at Dandio, one eyebrow raised slightly. "I have never heard of a serpentine speaking," he said uncertainly.

"They rarely do—serpentines do not possess the intelligence to form coherent words. If it spoke, its master must have a very skilled grasp of how to control their minds." Dandio rubbed his chin thoughtfully. "Did it say anything else?"

"It wanted the sword—Drisilas. It said that a couple times, and then it started to ramble about prey and killing." A chill ran down Mel's spine as he remembered the rasping mantra, and he hurried past it. "It said it was trying to keep it from someone called Terrax. It said… the Dark One… wanted it."

That part didn't make any sense to Mel. But he noticed Llyrion glanced up sharply, and a look crossed Dandio's face that he didn't understand.

Mel took a breath. "I—I don't know anything more about the serpentine. I'm sorry we can't help more," he added. Suddenly, he felt reluctant to leave. Here he was among heroes, who seemed to be embarking on some sort of harrowing journey, and all he could offer was the monster's confusing message. Still, his responsibility to Misty—his little sister—won over. "We have to go home," he said.

Glentree frowned, looking at Rygal. "You didn't tell 'em?"

Rygal flushed slightly. "I—no, I didn't."

"Tell us what?" Mel asked, feeling a cold stir of fear in the pit of his stomach.

Glentree looked up at them, his brow creased with concern and pity. "Mel, serpentines are trackers. They know your scent now. It knows you're the last one with the sword, and it'll come after you again. You can't go home any time soon."

5

∽ ∽ ∽ ∽ ∽ ∽ ∽ ∽ ∽

Explanations

Glentree's words hit Mel in the stomach. The serpentine was tracking *him*. And now that it knew his scent, it would continue to pursue him until it either retrieved Drisilas, or killed him.

Or both.

Another thought struck him, and he looked up wildly. "But what about our parents? My mom got the sword from the market—her scent could be tracked too. She and Dad might be in danger!"

"No, Mel," Rygal reassured him quickly. "The serpentines, though smart, can only track one target at a time. While your mother may have been the first of your family to handle the sword, you were the most recent, and you are the one the serpentine saw with Drisilas. Their master, whoever that may be, is tracking you now, and you alone."

That didn't make Mel feel any better. "Then who sent the serpentines? And why didn't you tell us this before?" he added, sharper than he had intended. Instantly, he felt bad for the harsh tone. Rygal had saved their lives last night, both his and Misty's. He needed to be grateful for that. "Sorry," he mumbled.

Dandio spoke gently. "Rest assured, Mel, if your parents were in any immediate danger, I would return to Appledale to help them

49

myself. And while I hoped to break this news to you with a little more… tact," he threw Glentree a withering look, and the big man had the grace to nod an apology, "it is best you understand why things are the way they are."

"If I'd killed that serpentine, I wouldn't have brought you here at all," Rygal said. "But it got away, and by now it's passed the news on to all the others." He looked so disappointed in himself that Mel felt bad. But there was still something he had to know.

"You keep saying who the serpentines serve—that whoever it is, they're after Drisilas," Mel said slowly, looking at Dandio. "Who is it? And who's this Terrax person the serpentine talked about?"

Dandio nodded. "I will tell you—it's a long story, so eat some breakfast while you listen."

Mel and Misty gathered closer to the fire and sat beside Llyrion. The warm toast and savory meat helped calm his nerves. "Is there some way we can at least let our parents know we're okay?" he asked. "Could we send them a message?" He thought of the scattered furniture, the serpentine claw marks in the rug that his parents would have found upon returning home—

"I think that would be wise," Dandio said, nodding. "Glentree can ride back into town and leave a message for them."

"Thanks," Mel said to them. His mind still reeled, but slowly, he resign himself to the situation. If they were indeed being tracked by serpentines, the safest place for them was probably with Dandio. Another question came to him, and he looked up. "Wait—is it after Misty, too?"

"I doubt it," Dandio said. "Like Rygal said, they are single-minded creatures. Their minds are occupied solely by pursuing their target, and right now that target is you. Misty is safe."

"Then she can go home," Mel said. The words were barely out of his mouth before Misty protested.

"No, I'm not going home. I'm not gonna leave you, Mel! Mama always says to stay together." She looked at her brother seriously, her brow furrowed. She was right—if Mel and Misty went anywhere without their parents, that was the rule. *"Stay together, and keep your sister safe."* Mel could almost hear his mother's voice as she said it. Thinking of his mother made his throat tight, and he cleared it briskly.

"Okay. You can stay. If that's all right," he added quickly, looking at Dandio, who was clearly in charge. But the Liznee only nodded, and Mel thought he saw approval in his eyes.

Misty looked up at Dandio. "How do the serpentines know to track Mel?" she asked curiously. "And what was the one in our house last night talking about?"

"I will tell you, but we must go back a bit to understand our current situation," Dandio said. "First of all, about the sword. The flaming sword Drisilas, as you know, belongs to my brother the High King, forged by the hama-dryads many years ago. It is a powerful weapon, but useless in the hands of any other—only Ĵan can wield it. About three weeks ago, it was stolen by a man named Terrax."

Mel looked up curiously. "Who is he?"

Llyrion answered, his voice bitter with dislike. "An Elven outlaw, a descendant of Lord Liridox's line. He believes himself to be a prince, because of his lineage, and refuses to obey the Elimar Council as he should. Instead, he's been fighting against the Liznees and the loyal Elves for the last few years."

"Who was Liridox?" Mel asked. The name was vaguely familiar, and he regretted not paying attention in his history classes.

Misty piped up unexpectedly. "He was the first lord of Elvengate, remember, Mel? He had a whole kingdom and lots of money. But then Elvengate was destroyed, and that's when most of Liridox's descendants went southeast."

"Most of them, yes. But that was many years ago, and a story for another time," Llyrion said, nodding to Dandio.

Dandio continued. "Terrax wants both the throne of Caer Sia and the control of the Elven Council in Elimar. To get it, he has stolen Drisilas, presumably to bargain with the Liznees. But Ĵan thinks he is working for someone else, someone with more wealth and resources. We don't know who yet. At the moment, we do know that Terrax has joined with a rebel kragon named Adderstrike."

"A kragon?" Mel repeated, uncertainly.

"Great creatures from deep in the Magno Forest," Rygal said. "They are very intelligent, and up until now they have followed their king—who is allied with Caer Sia—quite faithfully. Until recently."

Dandio nodded. "Our sources reported that a few months ago, one of them left the Kragon Order and went rogue, on a revenge quest against the Liznees. He is called Adderstrike, but he had not yet appeared until he came with Terrax to take the sword."

Mel was bewildered by all this. A government of huge creatures, one of which had rebelled and joined with the outlaw Terrax…

Misty's face wrinkled in thought. "I learned about the Kragon Order in school—they're all supposed to be very loyal to their lord. Why would one of them go off with Terrax just like that?"

Mel looked at her in surprise. Apparently his sister paid better attention in her politics classes than he had at that age.

Dandio smiled at her and nodded. "A valid point, Misty. Actually, the situation with the Kragon Order is a little more complicated than that—they have a very complex government. To put it short, the alliance between Liznees and kragons is relatively new, established only a few years ago. A lot of kragons didn't want the alliance to happen, though—they claimed the Liznees had stolen their land. Once the treaty was in place, most of the protesters backed down—all but one. Adderstrike rebelled, and was banished from the Order. He and Terrax have joined forces now."

Mel looked at him as a new question occurred to him. "Hang on…how do you think Terrax and—oh what's his name, Adderstrike—plan on defeating Caer Sia? I mean, lots of stronger forces have tried that before, and it's never worked."

"Another good question," Dandio said. "Terrax is reckless, arrogant, but he is also cunning. He has seen the failed attempts of those who have tried to defeat Caer Sia before, and he has learned from them, each of them." Dandio counted off names on his fingers. "The Aces. Kado. Safacon. Each of them fought and fell. Whoever Terrax is allied with now—and as I said before, I assume it to be a person with some power—has made him confident enough to challenge Caer Sia again. However, compared to the circumstances, Terrax is not our main threat."

"What's the main threat?" Misty asked curiously.

Dandio stopped abruptly, and Mel had the odd sensation that the Liznee hadn't meant to say that last part. Rygal looked as confused and curious as he felt.

"There were… a few reports," Glentree started finally, looking at Dandio.

"We aren't sure if it's true at all, or if the reports were only rumors," Dandio cut in shortly. "Until we're sure, don't worry."

There was an awkward silence before Dandio spoke again. "For now, here is what we *do* know. Terrax stole Drisilas, then got rid of it to throw us off his trail. He is working for someone else—Jan and his advisors are currently trying to learn who that could be. Our mission now is to return Drisilas as soon as we can. There are other enemies, stronger than Terrax, who can twist the sword to serve their purposes."

A chill ran down Mel's spine. "What enemies? Do you mean whoever sent the serpentines?" he asked in a hushed voice.

"Maybe. I'm not quite sure yet who sent the serpentines, Mel," Dandio admitted. "But another threat is the Black Dwarves. We have reason to believe that they have also joined with Terrax and his employer—they assisted in stealing the sword from Sia originally."

"I thought all the Dwarve people were allied with Caer Sia," Mel said. He remembered that from his history classes.

"Yes, well, the Black Dwarves have never enjoyed being under Liznee leadership," Dandio said. "Like the rebel kragons, they believe our land is rightfully theirs and resent the alliance. In the last few years, groups of rebels have banded together in revolt."

From what Mel knew of Dwarves, they were dangerous warriors. And now it sounded like they would gladly fight anyone who challenged them. "What can we do?" he asked finally. "If we can't go home… what do we do?"

Dandio nodded. "Once the sword is returned to Jan, Terrax will retreat, and the serpentines will no longer track your scent with the sword. You could return in safety then." He stood. "In the meantime, we need to get going. The sun grows high."

Mel nodded slowly. Then, suddenly, he realized what this meant.

He and Misty had joined the quest to return the sword.

6

The King's Council
The same morning, in Caer Sia…

Allie Ki, daughter of Dandio, watched as Jan and Pellion Drona shuffled through the mountain of reports on their desks.

She had come originally to listen to the meeting—as part of her training, and considering she was the Crown Heiress to Caer Sia, she was required to observe official meetings as often as she was allowed. While these tended to be painfully dull, the excitement of the last few weeks made them something to look forward to. Besides, she had very little else to do. Her mother's mission in Badwater had been extended due to a few difficult dignitaries, and her father was away on a quest for the missing sword. So here she was.

Except almost nothing had been said so far, and she was beginning to feel bored and forgotten.

It had been Drona's idea to check the records of recent judicial cases. This would allow them to note down anyone who had a criminal history, and who might have also had reason to hire Terrax to steal the sword. The two men had sorted through reports ranging from murder to petty crime, anything in the last ten years that might give a clue. So far, nothing had been found of interest.

Drona straightened triumphantly, raising a sheet of paper. "Here!

The notes from last year's trial—if it were Farrell, he wouldn't be on this list…" He bent over the paper, eyes squinted, brow furrowed in concentration as he skimmed over the words. Then he sat back down, disappointed. "No, I forgot he was found innocent. Peter Farrell, of Cattrick Fief, North Daffodalion."

"He was a farmer, charged with stealing his neighbor's cow," Jan told him with a slight smile. "I would be surprised if he suddenly decided to hire an outlaw like Terrax."

"Are you certain Terrax isn't simply working on his own?" his steward returned, raising an eyebrow. "He may have banded with Adderstrike and orchestrated this on his own. Terrax never needs much motivation to stir up trouble, after all."

"I would think so, too, except for the fact that Adderstrike would require more payment than Terrax could have been able to offer him. Think about it. A kragon, deciding to join with an Elven outlaw just for the sake of it? I doubt it." Jan rubbed his brow, taking a deep breath.

Allie could no longer keep quiet. "Have you checked the Coonsian records of outlaws?" she asked finally.

They both looked at her, as if remembering she was there. Allie pressed on, brushing a strand of her wild brown hair out of her face. "Terrax might not be working for someone from Daffodalion, like you thought, Jan. Terrax is Daffonic, yes, but who's to say his employer is too?"

"That's what I was beginning to wonder," Jan admitted. He looked at Drona. "You suggested that Terrax would work for a Daffonic employer, because he would be more likely to trust someone from his country."

Drona nodded slowly. "It would make sense, sire. Think of how loyal Terrax is to his heritage. Why would he work for anyone who didn't support his cause?"

"Maybe if he was being paid enough," Allie suggested. "Then it wouldn't matter *who* he was fighting for. His reward would support his mission either way."

"Perhaps," Ĵan said thoughtfully. "Well, we have no access to the Daffonic criminal records beyond the last few years' anyway. I can send a message to King Micah of Daffodalion requesting to access them. In the meantime, we might as well continue to look through what we have."

"Sire, with all respect, who from Coonsia would you suspect?" Drona asked doubtfully. "In the last ten years, we haven't had a single outlaw with Terrax's type of strength rise up. Certainly none of them would have the right motives to hire him."

"Maybe not," Ĵan said, "but we might as well look."

He straightened stiffly. They had been at this for two hours, with almost nothing to show for it. No clues, no leads, nothing at all to suggest who had hired Terrax to steal the sword.

Allie folded her hands on the table, watching her uncle's face. "I can go to the library and bring back more records, if you like," she offered.

"Yes… thank you, Asescia," Ĵan said, lost in thought again as he skimmed over a page.

"Allie," she corrected him, but he didn't hear her. It proved how much was on his mind. Both Ĵan and her father had called her Allie since she could walk, mostly because her two-year-old self had been unable to pronounce *Asescia*. Jan only called her that when she was in trouble, or when he was worried.

In this case, she could tell it was the latter.

She walked down Castle Sia's halls, weaving her way past servants or courtiers, a slightly built Liznee girl of seventeen. Most of the groups moved out of her way. Being the Crown Heiress had some advantages, she thought wryly as she reached the royal library.

It was a large, dimly lit room made up of towering shelves upon which were stored books of all kinds. The shelves closest to the door contained books of fiction, where legends and mythologies were compiled in volumes, beautifully scripted by their authors.

Further back, she found the shelves where the official records were kept. Allie scanned the spines of the books until she found the one she needed, removed it from the shelf, and started back down the halls to the council room.

"Perhaps the Kragon Order holds more dissension than we were led to believe," Drona was saying as Allie re-entered the room. "Perhaps Adderstrike is not the only rebel. Their lord has some wealth. He could easily hire Terrax to undermine your authority." He paused. "And think, they have never trusted the Liznees."

"Indeed," Jan said, rubbing his chin. "But it's no small thing to accuse our allies of treason."

"I don't suggest you do, sire," Drona said crisply. "I only recommend we analyze all possibilities. It might be worth sending a… cautionary message to Lord Fireclaw."

Jan thought for another moment, then his face cleared as a

thought occurred to him, and he stood. "You're quite right. Allie, bring me a piece of paper and a quill, will you?"

Allie set the book down on the table, hesitated for a moment, then, knowing she would get no answers from her uncle until he got what he needed, moved to the shelf on the wall where sheets of parchment and quill pens were kept.

"What—what are you doing, sire?" Drona asked, just as confused as Allie.

Jan took the pen and paper, looking almost cheerful. "Pellion, you are truly brilliant. This way I can get my yearly meeting with Lord Fireclaw out of the way on the same day." He began to write rapidly.

"You're writing… to the kragon ruler?" Allie stammered slowly, the realization beginning to dawn on her.

"Drona is right—the kragons may have more news of both Terrax and Adderstrike," Jan said. "So I am inviting their lord to dinner."

7

᭦ ᭦ ᭦ ᭦ ᭦ ᭦ ᭦ ᭦ ᭦ ᭦

The Road to Tackert Fief

Mel's first opinion about quests was that most of the time was occupied by one activity.

Walking.

Lots and lots of walking.

The road they followed led them steadily west, with the gradually rising sun warming their backs. Tall maple and oak trees grew along the path, their leaves flushed orange and yellow with the coming of autumn and carpeting the forest floor. The road itself was wide enough for a carriage, and the deep ruts from wagon wheels told Mel that this road was typically well traveled. But they saw no other signs of travelers as they went.

The gryphon—Nella, as Dandio called her—padded on ahead of the companions, the breeze ruffling the strange combination of fur and feathers that warmed her body. Her head remained low to the ground as she scented the medley of tracks that marked the muddy gravel of the road. She reminded Mel of a very large puppy.

Dandio and Glentree walked behind Nella, talking quietly together. Llyrion remained near the back of the party with Misty, who had eagerly offered to lead the shaggy little pack pony. She took this responsibility very seriously, Mel thought with amusement, except she kept stopping to let the pony nibble the grass that overhung the road.

"Come on, Misty," he prompted as the pony paused to crop another patch of grass. Misty, disappointed, pulled the lead rope forward again.

"She's spoiling that horse," Rygal said with a grin. "He'll be too fat to carry the gear if we aren't careful."

"No, he won't," Misty said reproachfully, patting the pony's neck. Behind her, Llyrion smiled and lightly slapped the pony's rump.

"Better keep him moving, Misty. Once we get to Tackert Fief, we'll buy him some carrots, all right?"

Misty brightened at this and continued walking.

"What's at Tackert Fief?" Mel asked. "And how far is it?"

"We need to get supplies," Rygal told him. "We were going to do that in Appledale, but I don't think Dandio will risk going back towards the serpentines now. So our next option is Tackert Fief, about five miles south of here."

"South?" Mel repeated. "But I thought we have to go to Caer Sia." He remembered from his geography lessons that Caer Sia was in the northernmost corner of the country of Coonsia.

"We are," Llyrion answered from behind. "But the nearest town is Tackert Fief. After that, we'll veer northwest."

"Not like there's much at Tackert Fief," Rygal said, "but it's better than nothing. And we don't want to go all the way south to Lemsonburg, which would be our next option. Besides, Dandio says it's best to avoid the bigger cities anyway."

"Why?" Mel asked.

Rygal nodded at Drisilas, which Dandio wore slung over his shoulders. "Word spreads fast in big cities. The fewer people who know about our quest, the better."

Misty looked up, her brow wrinkled in thought. "Does Terrax have spies?"

"I would expect so," Llyrion answered her. "Still, there are others who would be eager to get the sword too, like Dandio mentioned this morning."

"Like the Black Dwarves," Mel said slowly. He looked up at Rygal as another thought struck him. "Why are they all fighting now? I thought everyone in Coonsia respected the High King's leadership—now it seems there's a whole bunch of rebels."

"That's complicated," Rygal said. He thought for a moment. "Have you heard about Safacon's downfall?"

Mel nodded. The name was vaguely familiar. "He was a sorcerer who took over Gayrile—he was defeated a couple years ago. You fought against him, right? How did you beat him?" he added eagerly.

Rygal grinned ruefully. "Yes, I was. We joined with the Direns and fought Safacon. He had created these Objects, of great power. The Jewel was the most powerful—it was made from a Star-Stone. Very similar to Drisilas, actually, but Dandio can tell you more about that. Anyway, Safacon was defeated, but his rebellion against the Liznees inspired a lot of people to do the same."

"Like Terrax," Mel guessed.

"Like Terrax," Rygal confirmed. "But he's had a vendetta against the Liznees for years—believes himself to be the long-lost heir of a city that doesn't exist anymore."

Mel was about to ask more when Dandio called back to them from up ahead. "Quiet down—there are wagons approaching."

The companions filed to one side of the road as two wagons, each pulled by two mules, rolled into view. The first wagon contained multiple barrels, Mel could see, and he could hear the sloshing of liquid from the inside as they passed. The other wagon had five passengers—two plump women with dark hair, a small boy around Misty's age, and two toddlers.

The driver of the front wagon pulled to a halt as they passed the companions, and looked at Dandio. "See any Dwarves that a'way?" he asked, in a lilting accent that blurred all his words together.

"Not that we saw," Dandio replied with a polite smile. "Where are you headed?"

"Gevari," the driver said with a gap-toothed grin. "We come from Tackert Fief."

"We a'have wares if you have pence," his companion added. "Oats, mead, and cornmeal."

Glentree slipped off his pack at a nod from Dandio, and fetched a handful of coins before moving to the wagon and inspecting the products with the first driver. The second driver remained seated, his dark eyes scanning the companions. "Where you a'come from?" he asked finally.

"Appledale," Dandio said. "We are going to visit family in Tackert Fief."

The driver eyed them as he chewed a blade of grass. In the cart behind him, the two women stared openly at the companions. Mel averted his eyes, stung by the scrutinizing gazes. This wasn't good. Rygal had said it would be best to avoid attention, and Mel knew word traveled fast through caravans like these. If word got back to Terrax that Drisilas had been found…

"Are there Dwarves near Tackert Fief, friend?" Dandio asked, his tone calm.

The gypsy driver turned his gaze back to the Liznee. "Dwarves, aye, quite a few from what we found. Seems they traveled that a'way not too long back, or so was said in the tavern."

"And we saw tracks," the younger of the two women added.

"Filthy creatures—think they own the a'whole world," the driver spat. "Well, I'd walk careful if I was a'you, Liznee. They don't take kindly to trespassers, an' you've got little ones with you." He jerked his head toward Mel and Misty. "That's the same reason we're heading back to Gevari."

"Indeed," Dandio said, voice thoughtful. "Well, I wish you safe travels."

Glentree moved away from the first wagon, lifting the now full saddlebags. The gypsies nodded to them and started off down the road. Dandio's friendly conversation and open manner seemed to have reassured them there was no danger. That didn't mean the companions were safe from gossip, though, Mel reminded himself.

"What was that about?" he asked Dandio as soon as the wagons were out of sight down the road. "What did they mean about the Dwarves?"

Dandio watched the disappearing wagons, rubbing his chin thoughtfully. "Are we well stocked?" he asked Glentree, who was loading the packs on the pony again.

"It'll last us to the border, at least," the big man replied.

Dandio turned his attention back to Mel. "There are several tribes of Black Dwarves in this area," he explained. "As I mentioned earlier, while most of them are allied with Caer Sia, some of them have joined with Terrax. From what that man said, it sounds like they're causing trouble near Tackert Fief."

"The gypsy didn't sound too fond of them, either," Rygal remarked.

"Yes, well, as he said, the Dwarves don't take kindly to trespassers," Dandio said. He paused, thinking for a moment. "We need to avoid a fight if we can. These Dwarves are radicals, but their people have inhabited these lands for centuries. It's not the cause that's wrong, it's the way they've gone about it."

"Knowing the Black Dwarves, it might be difficult to avoid a fight," Llyrion said doubtfully. Glentree nodded in agreement.

"Will we have to fight them?" Misty asked, wide-eyed.

Dandio smiled gently. "Not if we can help it. And I refuse to bring you two into any more danger than we are in already." He whistled for Nella, who stood on the other side of the road scenting the breeze. "Still, we'll pass through Tackert—I want to see if we can pick up any more news about the Dwarve movements. Then we'll continue our course."

They started walking again. Misty had moved away from the pony and was watching the gryphon, who padded obediently alongside Dandio. "Can I pet her?" she asked finally, looking up at Dandio hopefully.

Dandio smiled and patted the gryphon's neck lightly. "Of course. Nella won't hurt you. She's very gentle, in fact." The encouragement was all Misty needed, and she happily stroked the gryphon's fur. Nella gave a low, appreciative purr-like sound and turned her head so that Misty could fondle her ears. Mel smiled to himself.

"I didn't know you could keep a gryphon as a pet," he commented to Dandio curiously.

"Well, she's not exactly a house pet," Dandio said wryly. "I found her right after she hatched, at the base of a cliff on the northern coast of Daffodalion. I think she had fallen or been pushed from the nest." He looked at Misty with a smile. "Did you know that gryphons hatch from eggs, like birds?"

Misty nodded promptly. "The mothers lay a few eggs at a time. But the babies hatch only a day or so after. Faster than bird eggs, because with birds, the mama has to sit on the eggs for a while."

Dandio looked impressed. "Yes, that's right. You seem to know your facts."

"Only from books," Misty said simply, lightly touching the strange feathery fur around the gryphon's neck.

Dandio glanced back at Mel. "And what about you? What sort of things do you like to do?"

Mel thought blankly for a moment. It felt strange to think about his hobbies and past times—out here, on this journey, such things seemed almost nonexistent. "Well… I like being outside. Hiking and fishing and stuff like that. I'm not as good of a reader as Misty is." As much as he enjoyed stories, reading and school work had never come as quickly to him as it had for Misty. This usually made him feel self-conscious, and he was startled to hear himself admit it now.

But Dandio only smiled again and nodded. "Yes, that sounds a bit like Jan and I. I hated studies while we were growing up, meanwhile he was quite the model student." He laughed softly to himself, then looked ahead. "Well, we are nearing Tackert Fief. Stay close, you two."

Mel could see houses with thatched roofs ahead, and could smell the wood smoke. The road widened slightly as they drew close to the little village. "Dandio, if we don't need to buy supplies anymore, what do we need to do in Tackert Fief?"

"Nothing much," Dandio said. "But the news from the gypsies got me thinking. I'd like to see if we can pick up any more information about what we're up against."

8

Rumors in the Market

The chatter of poultry filled the air as the six companions entered the village of Tackert. Herds of sheep clustered along the edges of the road, bleating loudly. There seemed to be more livestock than people here, Mel observed.

He slowed his pace to take in the scenes around him. Crowds of farmers and peasants kept a steady stream of movement along the main road. The huts along the edge of town were small and simple, made of wood. As they entered the township, the houses and shops became slightly larger, made either from wood or tan-colored stone. There were no lamp posts to light the road, no signs marking the buildings. The entire village was a bland brownish-gray, blending in with the fading colors of the autumn forest.

People called to one another from booths and tents in the market. Farmers heckled over prices of animals. A group of small children played in front of the booths of the market.

"Like I said," Rygal said in a low voice to Mel, "not much here."

Mel didn't reply. It was odd—this town was less than a day's walk from his own, yet he had never been here. The poverty and weariness seemed to hang in the air. It suddenly made him grateful for his family's little home. "Do you think they'll have news though?" he asked in the same lowered tone as they passed by the little market square. In addition to poultry and sheep, booths had been set up to sell the last harvest of the season. Brightly colored squash and pumpkins were displayed by the noisy vendors.

"I'm not sure," Rygal said. "But you'd be surprised how many people pass through this town. It's the main road to get anywhere if you're traveling across the border from the southeast. And the gypsy caravans from Gevari are notorious for bringing in all the gossip."

A man herded a flock of sheep across the road in front of them, bringing Dandio's group to a stop. Mel took Misty's hand. The last thing he wanted was for them to be separated in the swirl of activity that filled the village.

Dandio motioned for the others to move to the edge of the road, then turned to face them. "Glentree, take the horse and wait for us on the far side of town. Llyrion, go with him, and then scout the forest on the west side. If there are Dwarve warriors causing trouble in the area, I'd like to know about it."

"What about us?" Misty asked.

Dandio turned to her with a slight smile. "I'd like you to go with Glentree and Llyrion. When you get through town, you can give the pony a few apples, Misty."

Glentree looked at him. "What are you going to do?"

"Rygal and I are going to stop in at the local tavern. We'll see if we can pick up any important information. Tavern keepers like to talk, especially if people pay well." A wry smile crossed the Liznee's face.

Mel felt a stir of disappointment. What Dandio and Rygal were doing sounded more interesting. "Can I come too?" he asked hopefully. "I want to help."

"I would rather have you away from town with Glentree," Dandio said, but he sounded thoughtful.

"Actually, Dandio," Rygal said as an idea came to him, "what if Mel and I went through the market while you went to the tavern? We could see more of the town and maybe hear some news or gossip. Plus, there are more people to talk to at the market."

"I did plan to scout the market after the tavern," Dandio said slowly.

"Might not be a bad idea," Glentree told him. "But your face is known here. Send Rygal and Mel, and you go get yourself a nice drink at the tavern and see what you hear."

Dandio finally smiled. "All right, let's do that. But be careful," he added to Rygal. "Remember, our mission must be kept secret. If Terrax finds out we foiled his plans to be rid of Drisilas, there could be trouble."

"I'm always careful," Rygal said loftily, grinning as he started across the road. Mel jogged after him, glancing back once to see Dandio hide a smile behind his cloak. In the dim light of the tavern, with his hood up to hide the distinctive scar, the Liznee could remain anonymous.

"What's our plan?" he asked Rygal softly. "Do we just wander and listen?"

"Pretty much," Rygal said with a shrug. He walked over to a table, where a man in a straw hat sold bunches of herbs. "Afternoon, good sir," he greeted the man with a smile.

"Afternoon," the vendor replied. "Can I help you find anything? Best herbs east of the border, these are."

"Lovely," Rygal commented absently. "Well, I'll take a bundle of rosemary, and if you could tell me where to get a treat for my little brother here I'd be much obliged."

The vendor handed him the rosemary, took the coins Rygal offered, and then motioned down the rows of booths. "They've got fresh pressed cider down yonder. I'm sure you'll enjoy it." He tipped his hat to them with a grin as they walked away.

"Are those really the best herbs in the area?" Mel asked skeptically as Rygal slipped the rosemary into his pack.

"Probably not—everyone says that," Rygal replied. "Still, we'll stay on the good side of these vendors if we buy their wares. That's how we get them to talk."

They reached the cider booth, where the fragrant smell of freshly pressed apples filled the air. Rygal purchased a cup for both himself and Mel, and they sat down in the shade of a maple tree as conversation and customers swirled around them.

"Rygal, I was wondering," Mel said slowly after a moment of silence. "What are you doing back on the Mainland? Did you come here after Drisilas was stolen?"

"No, actually," Rygal said. "At least, I wasn't in Caer Sia when the sword was stolen. I've been traveling back and forth between Gayrile and Caer Sia in the last two years or so, bringing information to Dandio. Since Safacon was defeated, we've reformed the Guardians up north, and Dandio wants to hear updates often."

"Then what are the Guardians doing now?" Mel asked, interested. "Now that Safacon's gone, I mean."

"Helping the public, forming alliances with people Safacon cut off, re-establishing trade routes…" Rygal shrugged and smiled ruefully. "I don't handle much of the political side of it—Norrin likes to do that, and he's good at it."

Voices, raised slightly in heated discussion, caught both their attention, and Mel turned. Three farmers, short and stocky, were arguing with the butcher. Mel studied them—their olive skin and dark hair and beards set them apart from the other villagers in the market. Their eyes were dark too, almond shaped in their broad faces. They were Dwarves, Mel realized.

"You gave us twice that much for the last load of mutton we sold you," one of them accused the butcher. His voice was slightly rasping, with a heavy accent.

"Right, well, in light of recent events, I can't in good conscience buy for that price," the butcher reiterated. "My own dear mother lost half her flock of hens last night—stolen, they was, by the rebels."

"Our tribe has no dealing with those traitors," the Dwarve farmer snapped. "We're loyal to the king, just as you should be to yours."

"This isn't Coonsia. You're in Daffodalion still—and Tackert Fief has suffered heavily from your people in recent days," the butcher informed him flatly. "I'll give you a lupin for the whole load—take it or leave it."

The Dwarves talked amongst themselves for a moment, then took the proffered coin with a scowl and handed the packages of mutton over to the butcher.

"Come on," Rygal said quietly, and moved to follow the Dwarves. Mel followed curiously. Dandio had mentioned that the Black

Dwarves were causing trouble, but he didn't think these Dwarves fit into that category. They just seemed to be trying to make a living.

"Excuse us, gents," Rygal called, causing all three Dwarve farmers turn to them. Now that they were up close, Mel could study them better. Fully grown, they were barely taller than he was. Each of them carried a simple wide-bladed knife at his belt, and their beards were braided with beads. Their expressions held no trace of fear— they just looked tired and exasperated.

Rygal spread his hands in a placating gesture. "I don't want to argue, I just have a question. I take it you're not with the rebel tribes."

The Dwarve who seemed to be the leader folded his burly arms over his chest. "No, we are not. What're you doing this far south, Garilian? You're a long way from home."

Rygal ignored the hostile tone and smiled. "I didn't think you were. We wondered if you have any news about the movements of the rebels. We are traveling north and we don't want to cross paths with them."

One of the other farmers scowled at him. "We might not be with them, but we aren't in the business of betraying our countrymen, Parder," he said to the leader.

"Shut it, Hackam," the first Dwarve, Parder, ordered shortly. He studied Rygal carefully, his dark eyes scanning him up and down. "Why do you want to know?"

"I'm with the Guardians of Gayrile," Rygal said quietly. "We don't mean you or your tribe any harm. But these rebels are dangerous— and we need to know if you have any information."

The Dwarve leader nodded slowly. "I thought as much. We've

heard of the Guardians, at least. But we don't have any news about the rebels. I'm sorry."

"Are you sure?" Mel said before he could stop himself.

The one called Hackam looked at him. "Like he said, we have no doing with them. And they want nothing to do with us."

"There are rumors that they are near the North Gully, which is not far from here," the third Dwarve said. "I would presume they are hiding in the caves. But that is a rumor only."

"Not the worst one we've heard either, if you recall," Hackam muttered. His companions threw him looks, and he grew quiet.

Rygal looked at him with a slight frown. "Not the worst… rumor? What do you mean?"

"Now see what you've done, Hackam?" the third Dwarve berated his friend under his breath.

The Dwarve called Parder glanced at his companions, then met Rygal's eyes again. "Never mind. We might as well pass it on to you—see what you make of it. My friend here, Tarlin," he nodded to the third Dwarve farmer, "heard a strange thing in town only yester-morn, a story of serpentines headed north. They had been given a mission, their minds controlled. Someone with great strength would have to do this, you understand," he added to Rygal.

"Yesterday… that was my birthday, Rygal," Mel said, realizing what this meant. "They must have seen the serpentine that came to Appledale."

"You've seen it, then," Parder said, sounding interested. "Well, thank your gods you're still here. But that's not it. The same day, we heard tell of another danger, a shadow from long ago. Its powers have already affected the forests to the east, we have heard. Trees decayed and dying long before their time, and the dryads fleeing east to escape it. It is a thing we do not understand, but fear greatly." He hesitated. "We believed it gone, but now we can assume…"

He trailed off, as if unable to finish his own thought. Mel looked at the three Dwarves in confusion. Each of their faces reflected fear and uncertainty that he didn't understand. They weren't afraid of the serpentines… this was something different.

"Assume what?" Rygal prompted slowly.

Parder still hesitated, and his companion Hackam met Rygal's eyes. "Assume that the Darkness has returned," he said quietly.

The words meant nothing to Mel, but the Dwarves' faces were pale. The dread in their eyes at Hackam's words seeped into Mel's core. "The… Darkness?" he repeated, voice hushed, and looked up at Rygal.

Rygal was still frowning slightly, but now it looked like he was thinking hard. "Thank you for telling us this," he said to the farmers. "I'll pass that news along as well. Keep your tribe safe. We don't want them to get involved in a fight."

Parder nodded. "Very well. Travel safe, Garilian." The three Dwarves bowed slightly, then turned to follow the thin winding trail into the forest.

"Come on, Mel," Rygal said, and then started down the main road in the opposite direction. They walked through town

Mel looked up at him, totally confused. "Rygal, what were they talking about? What's…" he lowered his voice, "the Darkness?"

"I don't know," Rygal admitted quietly. "But Dandio probably will. Either way, I'm starting to guess what's going on—and why the serpentines are after you."

Mel tripped over a tree root that overgrew the trail outside town, but he barely noticed. Rygal's words had caught his attention. "Really? Who do you think…" he trailed off uncertainly.

"Glad you two made it back," came Glentree's voice. The burly warrior stood in a small clearing just off the road. He had set up the tents, and built a small fire. Misty sat by the campfire, next to the dozing gryphon. "Llyrion is out scouting to the west."

Mel looked around, taking in their surroundings. This was the North Gully, he gathered, or at least the entrance to it. The road dropped down slightly, so that the hills rose up around them, sheltering the camp from the weather. Further down, the road continued its gradual descent, and the hills became pockmarked with caves.

"Is Dandio back yet?" Rygal asked.

"Not yet," Glentree said. "Did you get any news?"

"We talked to some Dwarves," Mel said.

Glentree raised his eyebrows. "Well, Dandio will be interested to hear that. Eat something while we wait for him—we've got warm stew."

Mel moved eagerly to the fire. Misty stirred a large cast iron pot that hung over the crackling fire. "We made stew," she announced proudly.

The aroma of mutton and vegetables reached Mel's nose, and his mouth watered. "It smells great. Can I have some?"

Misty filled two bowls of stew. Mel and Rygal had just finished theirs when Dandio returned. Mel could tell from the tired, frustrated look on the Liznee's face that there would be no good news from him.

"Barely got a word out of the tavern keeper," Dandio said as the others started to ask their questions. "So I waited to talk with some shepherds who arrived late. They had very little news, aside from local gossip." He sat down by the fire and dug into his bowl of stew.

Llyrion reappeared from the trees at the same time, carrying something on a piece of bark. "Something smells delightful," he announced, smiling at the others. "Any news in town?"

"Just a rumor that raises half a million questions," Rygal told him, frowning at what the Elf held. "What's that?"

Llyrion held out the piece of wood to show Dandio. "Where we're camped currently is the doorstep of the North Gully. I scouted the forests to the west, on the other side of that ridge. There were Dwarve tracks aplenty, and I found this."

Mel stood to see. Resting on the bark was a cruel-looking arrow-head, smaller than average but with jagged, barbed edges. A strange silvery film coated the barbs.

"You found this where?" Dandio asked him, studying the arrowhead carefully.

"On the other side of these hills to the west. I didn't go all the way through the draw. Don't touch it," Llyrion added quickly to Mel, who had reached for the arrowhead curiously. "That's poison on the tips. These types of arrows aren't designed to penetrate deeply, but the poison ensures that even a shallow wound may be fatal."

Mel withdrew his hand quickly. "Where do you think it came from?" he asked Dandio.

"I am not sure. It could be nothing. But it may be wise that we alter our course east slightly, to steer clear of the gully caves," Dandio said. He looked over at Glentree. "If you two could try and find us an alternate route on the maps, I'd be grateful."

Glentree and Llyrion nodded and moved to the saddlebags. Dandio sat down by the fire stiffly, and looked from Rygal to Mel. "Did you two overhear anything of interest?"

"Yes, actually," Rygal said, leaning forward. "Mel and I talked to some Dwarve farmers. They didn't have much to report about their countrymen, unfortunately. But they had news about something else, a rumor about a… Dark Power." He hesitated. "I'm guessing whatever this other power is, it's the one that sent the serpentines. The Dwarves—they called it the Darkness."

The words sank into the silence that followed. A flash of many emotions crossed Dandio's face in a split second—doubt, fear, anger—it was gone in a flash, and his face was calm once again.

"Did they," he said finally, finishing his meal. His tone was level, without a hint of further questioning, that implied the conversation should go no further. Mel bit his lip, building the courage to voice his question. If whatever the Dwarves had spoken of was the reason he and Misty had nearly been eaten by a serpentine last night, then he needed to know.

"Dandio, what does that mean?" he asked. "Rumors and reports— what's the Darkness?"

Dandio's eyes were trained on the flickering fire, his face impassive. "I have already told you a little of it, Mel," he said finally. "Rumors only, that a dark thing stirs."

Rygal looked up. "What sort of dark thing? And why haven't you told us about this yet?"

"Because I don't believe in furthering rumors until they are confirmed to be true," Dandio said flatly. "The creature the Dwarves spoke of—we have thought it has returned before, and it turned out to be nothing. I have very little faith in the rumors of small towns."

"Then what was the point of wasting the afternoon there?" Rygal asked skeptically, standing. "I trust the Dwarves' judgment, at least. You know how skilled they are—they don't take rumors lightly unless it's an actual threat."

"Watch your tone," Dandio said in a low voice. "Our current threat is the Black Dwarves who have sided with Terrax. That was our mission today, to pick up news about Terrax, not to listen to local gossip."

"No, our mission was to listen for any news *of interest*," Rygal corrected him. "And if there's a potential threat, we need to know about it. Norrin told me that and so did you."

Dandio stood abruptly, facing him across the fire so that the yellow light played across his face. "Yes, I did tell you that. And this is what I'm telling you now. The Dark power that you heard about was killed. Years ago, with that very sword." He pointed sharply at Drisilas, which leaned against the saddle bags. "Worrying over every single rumor we hear of will waste precious time and energy. Our priority is getting to Sia."

"If it's dead, then why not just tell us?" Rygal challenged. "Or is everything you say about 'trusting your comrades' just a convenient excuse?"

Across the clearing, Glentree and Llyrion looked over in disbelief.

Dandio looked at Rygal for a very long silence. The look in his eyes sent chills down Mel's spine.

Dandio's voice was low and dangerous as he met Rygal's challenging eyes. "Sit down, boy. This is not about trust. This is a choice of judgment, and one that I will make based on my knowledge. Your choice was to would follow my lead on this venture. If you choose otherwise, I couldn't care less. You can either stay here and follow my orders, or go back north to Gayrile until Norrin finds you another local maniac whose head you can bust. Now sit down before I hear another word out of you."

His voice remained quiet, but the words resonated in the stillness. Rygal recoiled from each one as though he had been struck. He sat down again, his face white with anger. Dandio turned away and crossed to Llyrion, who quickly turned back to the maps.

There was a very tense silence. "I'll pack up dinner," Glentree said finally, clearing his throat. Rygal got up and walked over to set up his bed mat, eyes still blazing.

Misty looked up as Glentree sat down by the pot, her eyes wide. "Why is he so angry?" she asked softly.

Glentree glanced between Mel and Misty. "Can't tell you much more than what you've probably already guessed. What you heard today, lad," he looked at Mel, "that's not the first bit of news we've received about that particular evil. It's just the first time we've had to consider the possibility that the rumors might be true… and that's got Dandio in a fix." He shook his head. "Rygal ain't wrong though. You'll have to be told at some point," he added under his breath.

Mel looked over at Dandio, who was speaking quietly to Llyrion as they poured over the maps. Slowly, he was beginning to piece everything together. Dandio hadn't wanted to talk about the "other enemy" before, when he'd told them about Terrax. Now, the Dwarves seemed to have news of the same danger, and Dandio had dismissed this as well. What he had told Rygal—about how this Darkness had been killed by Drisilas before—echoed in Mel's thoughts.

Yes, he thought to himself inwardly. Whatever danger it was, Dandio knew it well.

He watched as the Liznee studied the maps, one hand tracing the scar that creased the right side of his face, a movement he usually did when he was thinking or worried. Mel realized in the same moment that despite all that he'd heard about Dandio Ki and his heroic actions, he had never known how Dandio had got that scar.

They finished setting up camp. Mel climbed under the tent beside Misty and curled up in his blankets. His mind was full of unanswered questions and worries. He watched Glentree cross to Dandio, and could hear their muted voices. He couldn't make out what was said, but he saw Glentree nod and move away to his bedroll by the fire. Dandio stood in the shadows, keeping silent watch on the camp.

Eventually, worn out by sheer exhaustion, Mel finally drifted off. His dreams were brief and confusing—serpentines chasing him and Misty through the house as his parents watched in silence, then the house dissolved around them and he was suspended in gray fog.

Someone was shaking him.

"Mel—wake up—hurry."

Rygal's voice came distantly through the haze of sleep. Mel blinked dazedly. "What—what's going on?"

From the look on Rygal's face, he knew it was nothing good even before he heard the answer.

"Terrax. Llyrion spotted his men on the ridge above us. For some reason, they've come back for the sword."

9

∽ ∽ ∽ ∽ ∽ ∽ ∽ ∽ ∽

Through the Gully Caves

Terrax. Mel sat up, all thoughts of sleep gone from his mind. Terrax had sold the sword and followed them from Appledale. Whatever the reason he was here now, Mel didn't want to wait around to find out.

"Where are they?" he asked finally in a whisper.

"On the hill above us to the east—we have to go before they trap us here," Rygal told him.

Mel shook Misty awake. She blinked at him sleepily, confused. "Get up, Misty," Mel murmured, his throat dry with anticipation of the coming flight. "We have to go."

Dawn was just arriving, turning the sky a deep purple and allowing a faint white light to reach the glade. Beyond the dense trees, Mel could see nothing. The rolling hills and ridges that surrounded the valley where they camped allowed for shelter, but it limited their vision. He peered up the rocky ridge above them, trying to see anything.

The two siblings shadowed Rygal as he moved toward Dandio and Llyrion, who stood in the shelter of an oak tree near the end of the valley. Dandio's keen green eyes scanned the hills above them. "How many?" he asked Llyrion.

"I'm not certain, but I'd guess ten or twelve men. They went right past my hiding place—Terrax was leading them." Llyrion fingered

84

the fletching of the arrow in his hands. He and Dandio were both calm. Of course, it wasn't a fight yet, Mel reminded himself. But he felt nowhere near as calm as they appeared.

Dandio turned to Rygal. "Load the gear on the pony, and be ready to run."

Rygal nodded briskly. He seemed to have put last night's argument with Dandio behind him in order to deal with the current situation.

Glentree held his axe in one hand, and in the other he gripped the heavy-headed mace. "We can fight our way out," he declared fiercely, the light of battle glowing in his eyes. "We'll make Terrax's band of ruffians pay."

"We can't charge into the woods with no idea of who or what we're facing," Dandio said, his voice level. "We could very well run into their trap. Terrax wants us to panic—that is exactly what we will *not* do. Is that clear?" he added meaningfully.

The others nodded. Rygal gripped the hilt of his sword. Mel had never seen him this nervous before, and it did nothing to ease his own fear. "What do you think we should do?" he asked quietly, as Llyrion continued his report to Dandio.

Rygal shrugged stiffly, his voice low as he answered. "Don't know. I trust Dandio's judgment here. But I don't like this. We're in a cage—all Terrax has to do is get a few half-decent archers up there, and then we're in a lot of trouble."

Nella growled, making Mel look up at the ridge. A line of warriors were silhouetted in the dim light, gradually edging their way down into the valley. He could see the faint glints of armor caught here and there by the slowly rising sun, the flash of a sword half-drawn in a scabbard, or an axe slung over a shoulder.

"Dwarves." Llyrion swore under his breath. "Dandio—they're Dwarves."

A second group had appeared on the ridge behind them, and were steadily moving down. Mel felt his heart rate quickening. They were in a vice—soon, they would be trapped.

Dandio stepped forward suddenly. His cloak rippled in the slight breeze, and red light glowed in his hands as he addressed the new-comers. "Stop. Why do you come here?" His voice carried over the valley, and the warriors paused.

The voice that answered was not a Dwarve's—it was similar to Llyrion's, but with a stronger accent, and a cruel tone. "Ah, so it's true then. Dandio Ki left his safe little nest in Caer Sia to come after us."

At the front of the first group of warriors Mel spotted walked a tall, dark-haired figure. He was clad in tarnished silver armor, his cloak tattered, and there was an unkind light in his cold blue eyes. His pointed ears and accent marked him as an Elf. Llyrion clipped an arrow to the string, his face darkening in anger as he saw the stranger.

Dandio's voice was still calm. "Don't flatter yourself, Terrax. I didn't come looking for you, or your gang of criminals, for that matter. But you haven't answered my question—why come you here?"

Terrax drew a long, lean knife and pointed it, abruptly, at Mel. "Him," the Elven outlaw said bluntly, as Mel flinched back reflexively. "That boy has tampered with things he knows nothing about. And now you have only made things worse for him by bringing him into this, Dandio."

"He was only 'brought into this', as you say, because of your arrogance," Dandio replied curtly. "Now, if you have nothing further to say, leave. I have no wish to fight you."

"None ever do," Terrax said sarcastically. "Especially when you are outnumbered. That is why I give you this chance to surrender the sword to me."

"And what use can you have of Drisilas now?" Dandio asked with a slight frown. "Terrax, you know you cannot hope to wield it. Why risk the lives of your men for it at all?"

The Dwarve warriors had entered the valley and stood behind Terrax. Their dark eyes held a hateful and dangerous light that was very different from the expressions of the peaceful farmers Mel had met yesterday. These Dwarves had come for blood.

Terrax raised his chin. "I have learned of the sword's true powers. To gain them, I do not need to wield it. I need only take the stone—a stone that rightfully belongs to my people. We were slighted, lied to long ago." He gestured to the Dwarves behind him. "The Liznees lied to the Dwarves too—robbed them of land that was rightfully theirs. They are ready to fight for it now."

The line of Dwarves and outlaws edged closer. Dandio's green eyes rapidly analyzed the situation. Mel had no idea how they would escape this. They were outnumbered ten to one.

The tense silence ended as one of the Dwarve warriors, self-control broken, flung a dagger at Dandio. The Liznee swayed out of the way in the same moment that Llyrion's arrow slammed into the chest of the offending warrior. Terrax shouted, and in another second, battle had begun.

Dandio extended his hands. Crackling red fire shot from his fingertips and struck the approaching warriors. Several of them fell back under the Liznee's power. "Go!" Dandio ordered, and the companions ran, sprinting toward the valley end. Mel gripped Misty's hand as they ran. His heart pounded so loud he was sure everyone could hear it. Behind them came the clang of steel on steel, screams from Terrax's warriors, pounding feet—

He risked a glance back and felt his stomach lurch as he saw the Dwarves coming after them. They were pointing at something, and he realized they had spotted Drisilas, strapped to Nella's saddle bags. Rygal led the pack pony ahead while Nella trailed behind. The gryphon was snarling, clearly eager to attack the pursuing Dwarves, but Rygal shouted a command, and she followed obediently.

For a moment, Mel wondered if they could simply fly to safety on the gryphon. The thought was banished just as quickly. They wouldn't all fit on Nella—and clearly, no one would be left behind.

Dandio joined them at the mouth of the stone tunnel—the first onslaught of outlaws and Dwarve warriors had been slowed, most of them laying on the ground, nursing wounds and groaning in pain and rage. The sudden violence and the Liznee's rapid counter attack reminded Mel how glad he was that Dandio was on their side. "We need to go up there," Dandio panted as he reached them, pointing ahead. "The caves—it'll be the fastest way out of here. We can follow the tunnels and emerge on the other side of the gully."

Llyrion nodded, and took Mel's arm. "Come with me and stay close. It's a maze in there."

"Llyrion—what does Terrax want with me? Why does he want the sword back?" Mel gasped as they entered the tunnel. Misty stumbled over a rock and fell as Mel pulled her along.

"He wants Drisilas—for what purpose I don't know, but either way his plans for the sword to disappear have been foiled," Llyrion explained. "Didn't expect the Darkness to send the serpentines and get involved, I suppose," he muttered to himself.

But Mel heard, and looked at him in shock. The Dark Power that Dandio was so fearful of—had sent the serpentines? "What?" he stammered.

"I'll tell you later, I promise. Whatever Dandio says, you deserve to know," Llyrion said grimly. "But right now we have to get out of here."

They ran through the winding tunnels. Llyrion seemed to know the tunnels well. Or he just had a really good sense of direction, Mel thought. He was disoriented in the first few minutes. The light faded, and Llyrion paused to light a torch. Up ahead, Mel could see Glentree and Rygal, moving uncertainly and carrying a second torch. He heard the anxious whinny of the distraught pony, who objected strongly to the narrow confines of the tunnel. Dandio remained in the rear, covering the retreat. The glowing red fire he wielded in his hands lit his way.

They reached Rygal and Glentree, who both looked lost. "Which way?" Rygal asked anxiously. He was out of breath, gripping his sword tightly in one hand, and holding the pony's lead rope in the other.

"Come on," Llyrion said, leading them onward. They wove through the blackness, bumping into sharp stones, the uncertain light playing tricks on their eyes.

That was when a hand gripped Mel's other arm and hauled him down, off the main road they were following. Misty's little hand was torn from his grasp as a Dwarve dragged him off the trail and down into darkness.

"Hey!" Mel tried to shout, but the cry was cut off as a second hand clamped over his nose and mouth. He couldn't breathe as the Dwarve warrior forced him to the ground, the hard rocks digging into Mel's chest and face.

Then there came a flash of red—Dandio. The Liznee dropped down beside them, sending the Dwarve retreating rapidly, and knelt by Mel. "Are you hurt?"

Mel gasped for breath. His stomach lurched from the horror of the encounter. "No," he managed to wheeze.

Dandio gripped his arm, and they made their way back up onto the main path. Torchlight came faintly from ahead—Mel tripped over something soft, and looked down. A Dwarve warrior lay on the path, one of Llyrion's arrows embedded in his chest. Again, his stomach lurched, and he looked away hurriedly as Dandio urged him forward. More bodies lay on the stone floor as they walked toward the light, some with wounds from a sword, others with Llyrion's deadly green-feathered arrows, others battered and disfigured by Glentree's powerful axe and mace.

The other four companions whipped around warily as Dandio and Mel approached. Llyrion lowered his bow immediately. "Are you all right?" he asked Mel quickly.

"Yeah…" Mel studied them all. Rygal had a shallow cut across his forearm, and Glentree's burly arms were scoured with small scrapes and cuts. But no one seemed to be seriously injured.

"We must keep going," Dandio said. "The Dwarves know these tunnels better than anyone, and they will be after us again soon."

Mel took Misty's hand again. She was trembling, her eyes wide as she looked around. "It'll be all right," he told her, for the sake of saying something. Anything was better than this tense, painful silence, broken only by the noises made by the companions as they moved on as quietly as they could.

The soft footfall of approaching danger from behind was the only warning they received as the Dwarve warriors attacked a second time. Llyrion and Glentree both swung around to face the onslaught, swords flashing in the red light of Dandio's fire; Rygal urged Nella and the pony on down the winding tunnel.

Mel started to follow him, realized he would be mostly blind, and instead grabbed Rygal's hand. "Take Misty—put her on Nella, and please get her out."

Rygal nodded and lifted Misty onto Nella's back. "Wait, Mel—"

Mel stepped back. The terror gripping his chest made it hard to talk. "Terrax is after me. I'm not putting her in danger again."

"Mel!" Misty cried as Rygal started forward again, leaving him behind. An overhanging rock scraped Nella's saddlebags, tearing Drisilas loose, and it clattered on the ground.

Mel scooped the sword up and ran behind them, slower than Rygal's long stride, his mouth dry. Once or twice he struck his knees against the low-lying outcrops of rock. But he stumbled on, practically sobbing in fright, keeping his eyes on the rapidly fading light from Rygal's torch.

A hand gripped his shoulder, and he reeled back in panic. "It's all right—it's me," came Llyrion's voice. Mel squinted into the darkness. He could just make out the Elven warrior, his last arrow resting on the string. "We're almost there, Mel—come on."

They started forward again, feeling along the rocky walls of the tunnel. Rygal's torch bobbed up and down far ahead. Gradually, a new light reached Mel's eyes, ahead of Rygal's torch—daylight. Hope kindled suddenly in his chest. They had nearly made it—they were so close—

Then, out of nowhere, the road under their feet gave way and sent them tumbling down to the right, off the path, in a shower of dust and rocks. Mel rolled onto his back, sliding down the gravel into the shadows. It was pitch black. For an instant he feared he was alone, and panic gripped him. "Llyrion?"

"All right, Mel?" Llyrion called in the blackness.

"I'm here," Mel called back, feeling a surge of relief. He coughed through the dust. Llyrion's hand gripped his jacket sleeve, pulling him to his feet again.

"Road must have decayed along the edges," the Elf muttered. "Lost my last arrow—come on, we'll head back up this hill."

They moved slowly up the crumbling incline. The loose shale and gravel shifted under Mel's feet, filling his shoes with small stones. "Hear any Dwarves?" he panted nervously. The caves were suddenly silent. He hoped Dandio and Glentree had made it out.

"I think we've left them behind," Llyrion told him. They were halfway up, and a faint white light reached Mel's eyes.

That was when Llyrion stopped, listening. "Wait—quiet for a moment."

Mel stopped. He could hear nothing besides his own labored breathing and the pounding of his own heart. No sounds of battle or struggle, nothing at all.

But in the weak light, he saw the color drain from Llyrion's face.

"What is it?" he whispered.

Llyrion swung around, looking back down the way they had come. All Mel could see was blackness. Llyrion drew the short knife from his belt, moving between Mel and the shadows below. "What is it?" Mel repeated, his fear returning in a flash.

"Go," Llyrion whispered hoarsely, "run, run and don't look back."

Mel hesitated for a moment before he obeyed, running up the incline to the road. He heard Llyrion running behind him, heard the gravel crunch under their shoes as they reached the main path and ran toward the distant light of day. Dandio and Glentree, silhouetted ahead of them as they ran, reached the exit and vanished beyond.

"Keep running!" Llyrion shouted. "We're almost there, just keep—"

His voice cut off abruptly—Mel saw something out of the corner of his eye, a blackness darker than the shadows. Something swept past him like the flutter of great wings, and a breath of frigid air brushed his face, sending chills down his spine. Then the stone in Drisilas' hilt flashed a brilliant blue. The sudden light blinded Mel momentarily, and he tripped, grazing his knees on the rough path. Above him, he heard a low, angry hiss, and the shadows swept back like cloth flung by a sudden breeze.

He put his head down and ran the remaining few yards to day-light. The tunnel opened out on a sloping hillside—he slid down the slope, feet skidding in the slate and gravel. The forest stretched on beyond the tunnel mouth. His companions stood breathless in a sun-lit glade just below. Mel crashed into Rygal, who stood by Nella. Misty sat safely on the gryphon's back.

"There you are," Rygal breathed in relief. "Where's—"

Then he stopped abruptly, looking back. His face wrinkled in confusion—then worry.

Llyrion appeared from the tunnel mouth, stumbling. Then he fell to his knees and rolled down the hillside to lay on his back, unmoving, in the soft grass.

They rushed forward at once, but Dandio reached him first, dropping to his knees beside the fallen Elf. The expression on his face chilled Mel to the bone. It was an expression of total helplessness, and it didn't seem right on the face of such a legend. "Glentree, get the medical kit," he ordered shortly.

Llyrion coughed, a horrible rattling sound, like a breath of ice. "Can't—I can't—Dandio—" His voice was weak and rasping.

"He's unscathed," Rygal said hoarsely. "Not a mark on him."

Mel remained by the gryphon, unable to move. He hugged Misty's head into his chest so that she wouldn't see, but he could see every-thing from his place. Llyrion's face was deathly pale, and his chest rose and fell, slowly and weakly, as the very life seemed to drain from him.

Dandio's skilled hands sought for a wound, but Mel realized Rygal was right. There was no blood, no broken bones, no mark where an object could have struck.

"What happened?" Dandio asked, looking directly at Mel.

"I—we fell off the path, not very far—I didn't see anything—he told me to run," Mel stammered. His words tumbled out in a rush, fear and desperation and helplessness in every syllable.

"Dark," Llyrion whispered, and swallowed hard; he was shivering, his lips tinged blue. "It—was dark—cold—Dandio—it's back—it's come for the sword—"

"It's all right…you'll be all right…hold on…" Dandio murmured to him, loosening the top of the Elf's jerkin and folding down the collar. What looked like a large dark bruise had appeared directly under his jaw. Dark lines ran down Llyrion's neck, seeping into the veins.

Mel knew, somehow, that there was no way to treat that kind of wound.

"Light above," Glentree murmured dully.

Dandio straightened, laying a hand on the Elf's shoulder. Llyrion met his eyes, clearly reading the message there. But Mel was surprised by the calm on the Elf's face as he smiled up at his leader. "Dandio—Linwy and Alder—please keep them safe," he whispered hoarsely. He coughed again, and rasped something else, faintly. Dandio bent over him, listening. The Elf gathered his strength, then spoke again.

"Go."

"Llyrion…" Rygal said wretchedly, kneeling beside Dandio.

Llyrion's face was calm, his eyes clouded. His rasping breaths slowed before finally stopping.

He was gone.

Dandio rested his head briefly on the Elf's still chest. Glentree and Rygal knelt beside their fallen comrade, tears wetting both their faces. Mel held Misty tightly; he could feel her trembling with sobs, and realized he was crying too, silent tears that left bright trails on his dusty face.

There was a long, painful pause before Dandio straightened and spoke quietly. "We're heading north. I no longer trust this road. I was a fool—may the Light reward me in full for this," he added bitterly, then turned to Rygal. "Load the gear evenly between Nella and the pony—I need them both to travel at the same speed. We must hurry."

"What…what about him?" Rygal asked. He sounded much younger.

"I will tend to him," Dandio replied softly. His face was gray, voice dull. Every part of him had been shaken by the loss. Even Mel, who had only been with them for a few days, who really didn't know much about these things, could understand that.

Birdsong filled the wood again as they started north.

10

A Story at Sunrise

They traveled the rest of the day and into the night. Dandio was determined to keep moving. Their original road had been abandoned; now they traveled due north. The land sloped up in a series of steep hills as they left the gully behind, so that they were left toiling uphill through the soaking underbrush.

Right around nightfall, they turned west gradually, moving through the trees. The path became harder to see, and Mel wondered how long they would travel. His feet were beginning to hurt, and he was soaked through. But he didn't venture to voice his complaint, not after the day's events. Dandio led them onward, tall and silent.

No one spoke on the journey.

A few hours after dusk, Dandio finally called a halt, mostly because Misty was falling asleep as they walked.

"I can keep carrying her," Mel offered, holding his little sister tightly. He didn't want them to be the cause for stopping.

Dandio let out a long breath as he saw them. "No…no. We'll stop for the night. We are all tired."

Misty squirmed out of Mel's arms, rubbing her eyes stubbornly. "No, I can keep walking. I don't want to make you upset." She looked up at Dandio with wide eyes.

The Liznee's face softened, and he knelt down in front of her as the others began setting up the camp. "I'm not upset with you. Not at all. You are—both of you," he added, looking at Mel, "doing very well. And none of what happened today—none of it—is your fault."

Mel looked down, his throat tight. "I wish I could have helped," he mumbled, though he knew there was little he could have done.

"I wish the same," Dandio said quietly, and Mel realized he was talking about himself. He looked up as the Liznee moved away, watching as he spoke with Rygal.

The shock of the day and the long walk had drained Misty entirely of energy, and within a few minutes of laying down, she was asleep. Mel could hear her murmuring faintly in her sleep, most likely reliving the day's horrific events in her dreams. The tent felt too tight and cold, and he moved his mat beside the fire.

It was colder outside, but the crisp air was refreshing somehow. His thoughts strayed to Llyrion as he lay there, and fresh tears burned behind his vision. He swallowed hard and looked over at Rygal, who had settled down across the fire and wrapped himself in his cloak. Glentree unloaded the gear from the faithful little pony and gave Nella a drink of water. Across the clearing, Dandio stood on watch.

"How far are we from Coonsia, Rygal?" Mel asked softly, mostly for the sake of conversation.

"Not far," came the reply. "It might be a little longer now, though. We took a different route than we were originally planning, after..." he trailed off. Neither of them seemed ready to talk about Llyrion.

"Is...was there anyway..." Mel started, not sure how to put it. He knew, from the stories he'd heard, that when someone was injured, the person's companions could often find herbs or some other way of healing even in the wilderness. Dandio was experienced enough to know exactly how to treat different wounds, which meant that Llyrion's hadn't been one you could treat with medicine…

"There's nothing in Orlell that could have helped an injury like that," Glentree said softly, staring into the fire.

Rygal looked at him. "Then…you know what killed him?"

"We'll talk about it in the morning. Get some sleep," Glentree told them briskly. Knowing he would get no more answers from him tonight, and not sure if he wanted to talk about it anyway, Mel rolled himself in his blankets and lay silent. It took him a long time to fall asleep. The terrifying scenes of the day replayed over and over in his head. The hate and fire in Terrax's eyes, the Dwarve pulling him into the darkness, Llyrion running with him towards the distant light— and then Llyrion on the ground, lifeless, killed by an unknown foe…

What *had* killed him?

He closed his eyes and allowed himself to sink into sleep. But even in his dreams, terror pursued him, and he woke feeling groggy.

The sun had just risen, filling the camp with morning light. Mel looked around briefly. Dandio stood in the same place he had been last night, watching the woods. Mel doubted he had ever gone to sleep.

He got up, rolling up his bed mat, a little surprised by how late in the morning it was. Normally, they would all be up and eating breakfast by this point. Rygal and Glentree, on opposite sides of the fire, were still fast asleep, and Mel could hear Misty breathing deeply from the tent.

"Good morning," Dandio said without turning.

"Morning," Mel replied, not sure what to say. Even in the morning light, the pain of Llyrion's loss was still there. And there was nothing he could do to fix that. "I'll start the water," he offered finally. Hot drinks sounded very pleasant in the chill of morning.

Dandio turned and smiled faintly. "Thank you. Try not to wake Glentree. He can be very grumpy if you wake him up."

"I'm not asleep," Glentree mumbled, hearing only his name. Mel grinned at Dandio, and felt a sudden stir of hope that softened the lingering ache of loss. It didn't disappear, but the ache softened, nonetheless.

He filled the kettle and set it up over the fire, watching the coals glow. Dandio moved to sit by the blaze, warming his hands by the flame. "The good news is I think I know which way to take now," he said.

"That's good," Mel said, still watching the fire. That was one less thing to worry about, at any rate.

Dandio looked at him. "I owe you an apology," he said quietly. "For the night before last. It's not wrong to have questions, Mel."

"It's all right," Mel said quickly, feeling awkward. "I mean—you're in charge. And you've done this kind of journey more than we have."

Dandio shook his head. "It's no excuse. And now I see… you deserved to know."

The kettle began to whistle, which roused the other companions. They all gathered around the fire, quiet in the morning light. It was after they had eaten a small meal and sat in silence for a little while that Dandio spoke unexpectedly.

"Llyrion died a warrior," he said quietly. "I think you all know that. And I'm not going to tell you not to grieve because of that knowledge—knowing that changes very little. But I want you to each understand why things are as they are. Some of you," he glanced at Rygal, "have heard a little of this second power that is after Drisilas, which I mentioned before, however briefly. Some of you know very little. But…after yesterday, I think it would be best if we all knew exactly what we are facing."

Mel and Misty looked up, both interested. "I thought you weren't going to tell us about…whatever it is," Mel said slowly, not quite sure what to think.

"I wasn't," Dandio said, taking a breath. "But now with things as they are, I think it would be better if you knew. However, you should know that this isn't a simple matter. I will do my best to explain it…but I won't be surprised if you have questions and probably concerns too."

He paused. Glentree stood behind him, his burly arms folded over his chest solemnly. Rygal and the two siblings listened intently as Dandio began. "As you two remember, the serpentine mentioned that it served a Dark One, who wanted the sword. This matches a series of reports Caer Sia received just before Drisilas was stolen. Those rumors spoke of a great evil, an ancient threat reawakened."

"What is it?" Misty asked in a hushed tone.

The Liznee looked at her. "No one knows much about it. Nor, in fact, do we know the reason it wants the sword. It is simply called the Darkness. It is a wraith of blackness, a creature of ice and death, the greatest ally of the rebel Netrocrians who fled after the Dividing War. Before that war, the Netrocrians were meant to be guardians of peace, just as the Liznees and the Stars were. But their lust for power drove many of them to leave."

He hesitated for a moment, then continued. "Years ago, just before Jan became king, the human city Arkran sent us word that there was trouble in the Magno forest, a dark creature sighted in the wilderness. Arkran was our ally, and had been a pivotal leader in the Dividing War centuries earlier. Before we could aid them, Arkran disappeared."

"Disappeared?" Mel repeated.

"Destroyed," Dandio said. "A few survivors made it east to Tinkeeyo, and word reached Caer Sia telling of the attack. When Liznee scouts went to investigate, they found the city totaled, plants frozen stiff as if by sudden frost, and people dead and frozen in their homes."

There was a stunned silence—Mel and Misty stared at him, wide-eyed.

"What happened then?" Mel asked.

Dandio took a deep breath. "The Darkness was defeated a few years after that, driven back into the depths of the Magno Forest deep within Coonsia. Jan and I led that charge, actually—it was thanks to Drisilas that the Darkness was driven back."

"Drisilas?" Misty echoed in awe.

"Yes," Dandio said, nodding. He thought a moment. "When Drisilas was taken away from Sia's walls, the Darkness must have known. Its hatred of the sword and the Liznees was rekindled. It left its lair and began pursuing the sword, just as Terrax has."

"But Terrax doesn't have the sword," Rygal said, frowning slightly.

"No, not anymore. Terrax also knew the Darkness was stirring, and at the same time understood that it was far stronger than he was. So he got rid of Drisilas, in the best way he knew," Dandio said, and looked straight at Mel, "which placed the sword in Mel's hands, and fixed the Darkness' attention on Appledale. That is where the serpentine came into play."

"And that's why we couldn't go home," Mel said, beginning to piece it together.

"So…the Darkness is after us now?" Misty asked.

There was a long pause. "The Darkness is tracking the sword—it can sense it," Dandio said. "The magic that gives power to Drisilas and the magic that birthed the Darkness are related. The Stone in Drisilas' hilt—it came from the Star King, many years ago. That Stone holds ancient power from the Land Immortal itself. The Darkness seeks the Stone to destroy it, which would render Drisilas a mere blade. I would guess, to ease your minds, that its attention is no longer on your home."

That made them both relax. If there was going to be a battle, the last thing they needed was for their family and friends to be dragged in.

"Then how do we stop it?" Mel asked.

Dandio looked at him. "The Star-Stone in Drisilas' hilt is the only thing that matches the Darkness' power. That is why it is so important that we return the sword to Caer Sia. In Jan's hands, Drisilas is the best weapon we have to defeat the Darkness."

"What if it comes back?" Rygal asked, his face drawn with weariness. "What if the Darkness attacks one of us again?"

A familiar light flashed in Dandio's green eyes. "I'm not going to let that happen. If we are attacked, we will fight." He gave a half smile as he looked at Glentree and Rygal. "And there is not a single warrior in Orlell that I would prefer by my side for it over you two. Both of you," he emphasized, looking at the young warrior. The lingering hurt from the Liznee's sharp words a few nights before was driven out of Rygal's eyes by this confirmation.

Rygal's question had sparked another for Mel. "So… you think the thing that killed Llyrion was the…" He trailed off, unable to finish the horrible truth.

Dandio took a breath. "You remember we could find no injury on Llyrion, aside from the mark on his neck. I have seen that kind of wound… before. The kind of wound where the very Essence within has been destroyed. That's not something you can treat with medicine. The Darkness, following the trail laid out by the serpentines, tracked us into the tunnels, where I assume it encountered you and Llyrion."

Chills ran down Mel's spine as he realized how close he had come. He remembered the sweeping shadows, the way the sword had flashed as its strange magic defended him. "It's after me?" he said hoarsely.

"It is after all of us," Dandio said grimly. "It knows that Drisilas can bring about its demise, and so its one goal now is to destroy the sword."

There was a long pause.

"How do you know all this about the Darkness?" Rygal asked, looking carefully at their leader.

A flicker of grief—grief and fear, from some old memory—crossed Dandio's face, quickly masked. "Well…that's a story for another time. For now I think we had best get going. The sun grows high."

11

An Unexpected Meeting

The companions traveled west for the remainder of the day, moving at a steady pace. Oddly enough, the events of the last few days had bound them together in a new way—they were no longer merely companions who traveled the same path. Now they were comrades, friends, weary of the journey but hopeful of its success. The lingering ache of grief stayed heavy in Mel's heart, but he felt somehow that Llyrion would be glad to see how close the group had grown together.

Dandio worked tirelessly, hardly ever resting a moment and staying up most of the night even when it wasn't his turn at watch. Mel felt a stir of admiration for the rugged Liznee warrior.

Dandio also explained the importance of keeping the fire going through the whole of the night. "The Darkness is a Netrocrian, and thus a being that has no doing with fire," he said. "That's not to say that a fire will keep us entirely safe, but it's an extra precaution."

This was the second time Dandio had used the term *Netrocrian,* a word Mel didn't quite understand. When they started walking again, he asked Rygal about it.

"Well, there are three beings—three types of beings, I should say—that walk Orlell," Rygal said as they moved down the path. The road had become wider and better traveled as they had grown closer to the border. "The Cantrians are the most common—that's beings like humans and Elves. We don't shoot Essence from our hands at all, not like the Liznees can do."

"Then what would the Liznees be?" Mel asked, interested by this.

"Liznees are Fyrocrians—beings of fire. Their Essence takes the form of red lightning, which you can see Dandio fire from his hands. That power is essential to them, though—they only have so much at a time." Rygal sidestepped a root.

"And the Darkness?"

"A Netrocrian. Most of them are bad," Rygal said grimly. "Not all of them, of course—but most of them."

"I'm not sure I can remember all that," Misty said doubtfully from behind, her brow furrowed.

Rygal laughed. "You don't need to, but I thought I'd explain it. Llyrion had to remind me a lot when I first learned about it." His smile vanished at the name, and they fell silent, a cloud having come over the conversation.

And so they went on, one day following another, steadily heading north. It was the third day since the fight with Terrax when they came to a ruins of a great ancient castle. Silver towers, weathered and draped in ivy, stood crumbling at the edge of a wide clearing in the woods. A stream ran through the clearing, fed by a spring at the center of the rocky outcrop. A few purple flowers peeked out through the stones.

"Where are we?" Mel asked in awe as they stopped to refill the water flasks.

"This is Elvengate," Dandio said, his eyes taking in the scene. "The ancient city of the Elves. It used to be, at any rate—it was leveled during the Dividing War." He gestured to the ruined columns. "This is the kingdom Terrax hopes to recreate, if his mission succeeds."

Mel looked around. There wasn't much to build on, he thought. Still, there was a sort of majestic grace about the area that told him the city had been beautiful in its time. "What was the Dividing War, Dandio? You've mentioned it a few times now."

Dandio smiled slightly. "Years and years ago, at the beginning of time, all the species were united, for the most part. While they had their occasional disagreements, none was as great as the Dividing War. A group of Netrocrians—thousands of some of the greatest warriors the world had ever seen—rebelled against the High Light and the loyal servants. They, along with the mortals of Orlell who sided with them, fought for their land. Many lives were lost, and the surviving Netrocrian rebels vanished. But in the end, the loyal servants triumphed, and so Orlell was saved."

The story fascinated Mel. "So the Darkness came after that?"

"Yes, centuries later. It was believed that the Darkness was there in the Dividing War too, but it reappeared later, and that's when it destroyed Arkran just before attacking Caer Sia."

"It attacked Caer Sia? When?" Mel asked in surprise.

Dandio looked at him briefly. "It…well, it moved north. I'll tell you later."

Mel was left in thought as they began moving again. Dandio hadn't meant to share that, he could tell. The sadness in his eyes when he spoke of Caer Sia told of a memory too painful to discuss. The Darkness must have come to Caer Sia, which was likely how Dandio knew so much about it. Whatever had happened during that time, Dandio didn't want to discuss it, and Mel wasn't going to press him. But he was starting to guess.

By nightfall, they had reached a shallow valley in the dense woods. Mel noticed how the terrain had changed as they went further north. The tall birch trees and willows had been replaced by towering firs, the thick boughs sending the woods into shadow.

"How far are we from Coonsia?" Misty asked as Mel helped her set up the tent. Misty was the only one who slept in the tent now, nestled beside the packs. Mel had grown used to sleeping out by the fire, under the open sky, that he had begun to enjoy it despite the cold.

He frowned slightly in response to his little sister's question. "I'm not sure. Ask Dandio or Glentree."

Misty snuggled in under her blankets and yawned. "When we get there… we should send Mom and Dad a note."

"When we get there, we'll probably head right back home to them," Mel told her soothingly.

He walked over to the fire and sat down beside Glentree. The big man had watched the exchange with a slight smile. "She's a brave one, that one," he remarked.

Mel nodded. He was incredibly proud of Misty. She had followed along without complaint all this time, despite the dangers flung at them each day. "Are we getting close to the border?" he asked, reminded of Misty's question.

Glentree rubbed his chin thoughtfully. "Close, yeah. Maybe another two day's travel. By tomorrow we'll reach the crossroads, I'll warrant."

"The crossroads?" Mel repeated curiously as he set up his bedroll.

"This road we're on at present, it splits up ahead. When it does, we'll have to make the choice of speed or safety, but that'll be Dandio's call. He knows this area best," Glentree said.

Rygal sat down by the fire and frowned slightly. "What do you mean, speed or safety?"

"Exactly that. One road is safer, one road is faster." Glentree stood and stretched. "I'm going to unsaddle and rub down the pony—he could use a break."

Dandio walked over to the fire and sat down stiffly. He looked very tired, Mel thought. "Rygal, you and I have the first watch tonight," Dandio reminded him, and Rygal nodded.

"I can take watch with Rygal," Mel offered immediately. "You need a break too." So far, he and Misty had never been asked to take part on watch. He felt it was time he contributed.

Dandio looked at him and smiled slightly. "Well, thank you. Wake me at moonrise," he added firmly, then lay down by the fire. Within minutes, he was asleep.

Rygal shook his head. "*Wake me at moonrise.* As if we can't handle watch on our own," he murmured, grinning to himself.

"What do we do on watch?" Mel asked. From what he could tell, people took turns watching over the camp, and if there was any danger, they would wake everyone else up. Ever since the fight with Terrax and Llyrion's death, Dandio had taken most of this responsibility himself.

"Not much to it," Rygal said simply, standing and stretching. "You stay awake and watch for danger. Every now and then you patrol the camp, if you really want to."

"That sounds… kind of boring," Mel admitted.

Rygal nodded and shrugged. "It's watch."

They sat in silence on opposite sides of the fire, facing away from the camp, listening to the chirping of crickets and the cries of night birds deep in the woods. Mel's thoughts swirled restlessly through his mind. He thought about Terrax, of the story Dandio had told them about the Darkness a few days before, and of Llyrion. The pain of that loss was still fresh. The lingering grief had been replaced by a growing sense of guilt. He should have done something, anything more than running to freedom while Llyrion faced off with the impending death alone.

He took a shaky breath and forced the thought away. "I'm going to patrol," he told Rygal, who leaned back against a log by the fire. The young warrior nodded absently.

Mel moved to the edge of the circle of firelight, then moved along the perimeter of the camp. It was strange, he thought, that Terrax had tried to recover the sword from them that day. After all, if his goal was to leave Caer Sia unprotected so the Darkness could attack, then why suddenly decide to get Drisilas back?

That didn't make any sense, Mel thought. He pushed past a cluster of ferns, trying to move quietly, like Dandio did. It was very difficult in the dark woods. His thoughts returned to Terrax. Maybe Terrax hadn't known the Darkness was in the caverns. Maybe he just wanted Drisilas to use as a bargaining chip with Jan. Gain ransom or something.

But now that he thought about it, the whole battle in the North Gully made no sense. Terrax had deliberately misplaced Drisilas to reawaken the Darkness, or so Dandio's theory said. If Terrax's plan worked, it would lead to the Darkness attacking Caer Sia, and leaving Terrax with a throne. But if that were true… then what more did Terrax want with Drisilas?

He thought about the outlaw's words in the North Gully: *"I need only take the stone—a stone that rightfully belongs to my people."* The words had confused him, but judging by the angry expressions from both Dandio and Llyrion when Terrax had said them, they were important. If Terrax couldn't wield the sword himself, he clearly wanted it for some other purpose. Perhaps it had something to do with the Stone, then.

The pack pony nickered softly in greeting as Mel passed the two animals. Nella lay on her belly, head resting on her paws. Her ears and nose twitched as she picked up the many sounds and smells that Mel couldn't hear. "We should just leave you on watch duty," he told the gryphon.

Then, to his right, he saw a brief flash of movement.

Mel swung around quickly, scanning the woods. There was a small footpath that wound down the hill, back toward the main road they had come from. He squinted through the shadows, but could see nothing. Maybe it had just been a falling leaf or small animal, and his jittery mind had imagined more than there was.

Then he saw it. A figure, moving up the path toward them, going from shadow to shadow like a ghost.

Chills ran down Mel's spine. In the uncertain light it was impossible to make out any details. He ducked behind a tree and watched as the stranger approached. It appeared to be a human, he guessed. Whoever it was, he wasn't a tall man—only a head taller than Mel, maybe. He appeared to be wearing some sort of fur coat.

The stranger drew closer. Mel realized, with a jolt, that the camp behind him was now totally unaware of the newcomer. He realized he should have gone back to Rygal, instead of waiting to investigate, and kicked himself mentally. Now the stranger had started up the hill, and here Mel waited, weaponless and totally unprotected. The figure was almost to the tree where Mel huddled. Mel could make out no features, aside from a long mass of dark hair that was held back in a thick braid.

Mel shifted slightly, and a twig snapped under his foot. He froze in panic for an instant—and then the stranger spoke.

"All right, come out. I have heard your heart hammering away for the last minute and a half."

The voice was quiet, low-pitched, with a very slight rasp, and— most surprising of all—a girl's voice.

Mel peeked around the tree.

The stranger stood before him, crouched slightly, one hand on the bow slung over her shoulder. Her face was tanned, with pronounced cheekbones, an upturned nose, and vivid green eyes. Mel was so surprised he could barely form words.

She cocked her head at him, frowning. "Sorry to startle you. I've been tracking you all for days—finally caught up today. Is Dandio here?"

"Who—what—where—" Mel stammered, absolutely at a loss. And Rygal had told him keeping watch was boring—

The stranger sighed heavily. "Listen, I'm exhausted. I'm here with news for Dandio."

"You know Dandio?" Something clicked in Mel's mind, something Rygal had told him, about the quest to defeat the Hazes and Kado almost ten years ago, and who had helped…

Rygal's voice came from behind, sounding worried. "Mel? Mel, where are you?"

"I'm—over—here," Mel said haltingly.

Rygal pushed through the trees, and drew his sword as he saw the shadowy, half-certain stranger. "Get back, Mel!" He stepped closer, challenging the newcomer. "Who are you and what do you want?"

Mel saw the stranger's brow wrinkle. "Rygal?"

Rygal actually dropped his sword in shock, then peered through the uncertain light. "Good grief!" he exclaimed, starting forward again. "Is that—"

Mel moved closer to Rygal as the strange young woman took another step forward. Rygal stood stock still, looking her up and down as if he had seen a ghost.

"You got taller," the stranger said finally.

"So did you," Rygal returned. "Good grief!" he said again. "Dusty—how did you get here—what are you doing here?"

Behind them, the fire flared brighter, momentarily lighting the stranger that stood before them. As Mel had noticed earlier, her face was tan, the features not quite human, the eyes a far different shade of green than Mel had ever seen before. What he had thought to be a fur coat, he realized, was actually fur—she was covered from shoulder to mid-thigh in thick black fur, speckled slightly in places, allowing her to blend perfectly with the shadows of the forest. A thin scar creased her lip on the left side of her mouth, running at a diagonal down to her chin. Her ears were pointed, covered in fine velvety black. She wore a pair of soft leather shoes.

She straightened, back to business. "It's good to see you, but I need to talk to Dandio. Is he here?"

Rygal turned dazedly toward the camp again. "Over here. Mel, go wake Dandio."

The three of them moved back toward the circle of firelight. Mel jogged ahead, a hundred questions swarming in his mind. He was beginning to have an idea who the strange newcomer was—Rygal seemed to know her, at least.

Dandio sat up blearily as Mel shook him awake. "What is it? Is there trouble?"

"No, no, everything's fine," Mel said quickly. "Someone's here. She has news for you, apparently."

Dandio stood and stretched, then turned to face Rygal and the stranger as they approached. Mel saw surprise and pleasure cross the Liznee's face. "Well, look who's wandered in. You've grown, child."

"It took me days to find you," the other returned with a tired smile.

Mel could no longer keep silent. "What's going on? Who are you?" he asked, rounding on the strange woman, who sat by the fire, warming her hands by the blaze. "What's all this about urgent news for Dandio?"

The stranger grinned crookedly. "My name is Dusty, of the Mara-N'Tell Wildkids of Kasabren. We heard news of trouble in the Mainland—a Dark thing awakened." She glanced at Dandio, but he didn't comment. "We received word by the dryads that aid is needed. My people are currently providing refuge for those displaced by the unrest. But I knew I needed to get word to Caer Sia."

"Then why are you here?" Dandio asked with a half-smile.

Dusty looked at him—Mel saw a tiny flash of guilt cross her face, quickly masked. "I—my father sent me here. With a message for you and the Liznees."

"Well, let's hear it, then," Dandio said, sitting down.

Dusty hesitated again—Mel had the odd sensation that she was thinking fast. "My father—he said to tell you—that the Wildkids are ready to fight, if the need arises, and not to forget the old alliances with the Dryads."

"Is that so," Dandio mused. "So he sent you, then?"

"What? Yes," Dusty said quickly. "That is—he sent a message to King Ĵan—and he sent me on ahead of it."

"Because you thought you might find us here, possibly?"

"That's right."

Dandio leaned back against the log. "He doesn't know you're here, does he?"

Dusty opened her mouth, closed it again, and seemed to deflate. "No… no, he doesn't. But I heard that you were embarking on a quest to stop the Darkness, and I want in."

Rygal looked at her. "Hang on—you know about the Darkness?"

115

"Yes, doesn't everyone?" Dusty said, puzzled. "The Wildkids fought it, too, you know, centuries ago, before it headed northwest."

Rygal shook his head very slowly, looking at her open-mouthed. "Good *grief*," he murmured for the third time, this time impressed.

Dusty turned back to Dandio. "The Wildkids have heard strange stories from the west in the last few weeks." She hesitated. "I thought they were just rumors—but I trust the word of the Dryads. They… they say the Darkness has returned."

Dandio nodded slowly. "The Darkness has indeed returned, for what purpose we are not sure yet. I have seen its mark with my own eyes." There was a long, long silence in which Mel realized what was coming. "Llyrion is dead," Dandio said finally.

Dusty's face fell; she looked wildly around the camp for a moment. "What? No—how—how did he…"

"The Darkness attacked us three days ago, in the North Gully caves," Dandio said. His voice was dull. "Llyrion was killed as we retreated. The Darkness came in pursuit of the sword. None of us expected it." He stared into the flames, face expressionless, but Mel saw the pain and guilt in his eyes. "If I had seen the signs… if I had heeded the warnings…" he trailed off.

Dusty slumped beside the fire, her head in her hands. "They'll pay for that," she said finally, her voice hoarse. "The Dwarves, the Darkness, all of them—they'll pay."

"So they shall." Dandio cleared his throat briskly. "Well, then. You should know that the Elven outlaw Terrax has also sided with the Dwarves. He stole the sword originally, but now he seems to want it back—I am not sure why. There's quite a bit to tell."

Dusty smiled ruefully. "And I want to hear it, and tell my story, too. But I haven't slept in a day and a half. Maybe morning?"

"Of course," Dandio agreed. He stood. "I'll relieve you of watch, Rygal. The rest of you, get some sleep."

Mel lay down as Dusty settled down by the fire.

Rygal still seemed totally put out. "How did you even get here?" he stammered finally.

"Morning," Dusty muttered sleepily.

Rygal sat down, shaking his head. "I can't believe you're here. It's been years. Good—"

"If you say 'good grief' again, I'm going to stab you with an arrow, Rygal."

Mel saw Dandio smile slightly as he listened to the bickering. "Just like old times," the Liznee murmured to himself, then turned his attention to the shadowed woods.

12

News from the Kragon Lord
The following afternoon, in Caer Sia…

"Embassy approaching!"

The guard's announcement carried down to the courtyard, where the little group waited. Even from here, Allie could hear the fear in the guard's voice. An embassy of kragons coming to Castle Sia made her feel anything but comfortable.

She glanced at Ĵan, who stood beside her. The king's face was calm, impossible to read. His green eyes were fixed on the gate beyond, which would allow their guests to enter. *Guests*. The kragon lord and his courtiers, coming for dinner. She swallowed, her mouth dry at the thought of it. Allies or no, the kragons were terrifying creatures. It had been decades since a kragon had come to Caer Sia at all; even with the recent alliance, any meetings were typically done elsewhere.

"You can go inside if you prefer, princess," Drona said from behind her, which snapped her out of her thoughts. She flushed as she realized he had noticed her nervousness.

"No, I'm fine. Don't call me princess," Allie added lamely. Technically, as she was the king's niece and not his daughter, she wasn't a princess. That didn't change the fact that she was the heiress to the throne.

"Calm down," Ĵan said, hearing the tension in her tone. His low voice was so different from Drona's. Drona always seemed to speak too loud. "Remember, the kragons are here on friendly terms. We need any information they have regarding Terrax and Adderstrike, and this may be the only way to get it."

Allie took another deep breath. When Jan had first decided to meet with the kragon lord, she'd decided to come too, much to Drona's disdain. The steward had never liked a change in schedule, and he'd never really seemed to like her, either, for that matter.

Now that they were minutes away from the meeting, Allie was starting to regret her choice to attend. The idea of facing one of those creatures again was chilling, much less an embassy of them. But she was committed now.

Then, in a whir of mighty wings and flashing silver scales, the kragons arrived. Instead of landing on the lowered drawbridge and walking through the gates, which was what the hosts had expected, the kragons flew over the walls and landed directly inside the courtyard. Allie and Drona both took a half step back. There were four of them, three soldiers and their lord.

The castle's dining hall, though large, would never have been large enough to accommodate the kragon visitors. And so they had set up outside, in the slight chill of the early autumn afternoon. The servants, who for the past hours had busied themselves in setting up the banquet table in the courtyard, shrank back before the huge creatures. The kragons stopped before the long table.

It was the first time Allie had seen a kragon up close. They were massive creatures, with gray-green scales. Lord Fireclaw was easily identified by the band of gold on his brow. Well, if kragons had brows, Allie thought. The kragon lord hunched down, moving forward on the tips of his wings like a huge bat. His eyes were red-orange, the beak long and sharp. A frill of whitish feathers ran down the length of his spine, and flared behind his head like an exotic headdress. His tail lashed behind him as he moved forward, flanked by his three guards.

"King Ĵan." The beast's voice was a low rasp, reminding Allie of the cry of a hawk. The accent was exotic, lilting slightly, and making the W's in the words sound more like V's. "Honored ve are by this invite. Soldiers vill dine vit me, yes?"

"Welcome, King Fireclaw," Ĵan said, bowing courteously before the massive creature. "And yes, your soldiers are welcome to dine with us as well." He smiled to the other three. "I trust your flight here was pleasant?"

"Pleasssant," Fireclaw agreed, nodding his huge head. He spoke a word in the kragons' rasping, chirping language, and the three guards settled down. They dwarfed the banquet table, and Allie wondered vaguely if the cooks had prepared enough food. More importantly, she wondered what would happen if they hadn't.

"Please, sit, and let us eat," Ĵan said. He turned to his two companions. "May I introduce my advisor Pellion Drona, and heiress Asescia Ki. They will join us for this meal." Fireclaw's keen gaze swept over them. Drona bowed stiffly; Allie managed a nod and sank into her seat. She realized she had been staring openly at the four kragons for several minutes, and quickly adjusted her gaze to what she hoped was a welcoming smile.

"Meet you Fenkris, Harrstrike, and Kafrir," the kragon lord introduced his guards, who nodded respectfully.

Jan motioned to the servants, who stepped forward with the food. They bore two separate platters, each with an entire roasted deer on it, which they eased down to the table before the kragons. Then they carried out plates and silverware for the Liznees and Drona, along with their food.

They ate in silence for several minutes. Allie kept her eyes on the kragon lord, Fireclaw, who ate slowly. His strange eyes scanned the courtyard continuously, analyzing everything. There was an intelligence there and even a deadly cunning that told Allie it would be incredibly dangerous to get on his bad side. All the same… there was another light in the kragon's eyes, too. A deep sense of justice and interest in the whole matter. In a strange way, Allie trusted him. She knew they would have to, if this meeting was going to accomplish anything.

It was Fireclaw who spoke first. "Ve, you called here, for more den a meal, assume I?" he purred. Allie mentally rearranged the words so they made sense.

"Unfortunately, yes," Jan said, after a split second hesitation. The kragons were to-the-point, simple creatures. It would only make them impatient to go through the protocols that were typically standard in this sort of meeting, and so he began. "As you know, Fireclaw, the outlaw Terrax has recently stolen a weapon of great power from us. Besides that, we have reason to believe that he has joined forces with the renegade Adderstrike."

All four kragons hissed angrily at the name. "No longer of the Order is Adderstrike," Fireclaw informed Jan crisply. "He thirsts much for war. Two advisors, he killed them before he left. A traitor is he, and a murderer."

"Indeed," Ĵan said gravely. "Have you heard any news of him of late?"

"No. Strange I find it, that sided he vith Terrax. Unless great payment for his loyalty can Terrax offer."

Allie looked up, interested. So Fireclaw agreed with Ĵan's theory! If Terrax couldn't have offered Adderstrike anything to make him want to fight with them, then there must have been another who had hired them both… Someone who could offer enough to satisfy Adderstrike's greed and Terrax's motives.

"With due respect, sir," Drona said, clearing his throat, "what do you believe their intentions may be?"

"Not sure. This Terrax, he fierce. Great anger he has against the Elimar council." Fireclaw ripped a hunk of meat from the roast deer before him and chewed in slow silence for a moment. "But if sword he had, no use it do him."

Allie looked between Ĵan and Fireclaw. She was bursting with questions, but waited to ask them. What Fireclaw had said had set the gears turning in her mind. Terrax knew Drisilas would be useless in his hands. That was why it was so strange that he had stolen it in the first place—it was a move so risky that it couldn't have been just to spite the Liznees.

But then, if the person who had hired Terrax wanted Drisilas, then what was their motive? What could Drisilas do that other swords couldn't?

The answer hit her like a thunderbolt.

Drisilas was the only weapon in Orlell that could stop the Darkness.

Chills ran down her spine. She only knew a little of the black wraith that her father had spoken of only once or twice before. The Darkness, a shadow of days long past, a being of total destruction. The forerunner of the Master of Death himself. Jan and Dandio had defeated it years ago, with Drisilas. The Star-Stone in the sword's hilt gave the blade its power, pure power from the Land Immortal. Power entrusted to Jan decades before.

She realized Drona was speaking, and quickly turned her attention back to the conversation. "As the king and I discussed a few days ago, we doubt that Terrax could have anything that Adderstrike would value to entice him into joining him," the steward said hesitantly.

"Which is why I believe they have both been hired by someone else," Jan said, turning to Fireclaw. "An employer with enough wealth to hire them to do the dirty work of a rebellion."

One of the kragon soldiers growled something softly in his native tongue. Fireclaw turned to him, then looked back at Jan. Interest had sparked in his orange eyes. "Kafrir speaks of a meeting, between Adderstrike and Terrax, arranged by a second source. Mate of Kafrir overheard the rebel Adderstrike speaking of this meeting some time before his rebellion."

"A second source?" Jan repeated, interested. He looked at the hulking kragon soldier. "Sir Kafrir, did your mate overhear anything else?"

The soldier spoke again, and Fireclaw translated. "Mate of Kafrir heard very little else. Only that the meeting of Adderstrike and Terrax was arranged by this second source in secret. But heard she, that the one who arranged it had come from Caer Sia."

Allie looked up in disbelief. "Caer Sia?" she repeated out loud before she could stop herself. All eyes turned to her, and she took a breath to steady her nerves. "King Fireclaw, you know the history of Drisilas. You know what it's capable of in the right hands. What if the person who hired Adderstrike and Terrax—what if they're planning to awaken the Darkness again?"

Her question hung in the still air. She was stung as she saw the doubt on Jan's face, and the undisguised contempt on Drona's. "The Darkness is gone, princess," Drona said crisply. "Destroyed by the king and your father years before you were born, with the power of Drisilas."

"We didn't destroy it," Jan said quietly, and everyone looked at him. "We stopped it, sent it back to its lair in the Magno Forest, where it has stayed all this time. We received rumors that it had begun to stir again just before Drisilas was taken."

Fireclaw straightened. "What the girl has said, it is possible. This Darkness, ve have seen its power before. Robbed you of your only defense against it, Terrax has."

Jan started to argue, then stopped. Fireclaw's blunt words were all too true. "Until we know for sure that the Darkness has returned, we need to focus on the threat at hand," he said after a pause. "Thank you for coming here today. I trust I'll receive word from you if anything new comes up."

Fireclaw inclined his head in agreement.

After the kragons left, Allie sat alone on the drawbridge, watching the river flow by under her feet. In the silence of early evening, she thought about all that had happened. Drisilas had been stolen—but not to be used by someone else. It was used as bait. As a goad to awaken the Darkness from its long slumber.

She knew little of the wraith that her people so feared, and made a mental note to ask Ĵan about it in the morning. Dandio had never told her much about it. She thought about her father, somewhere out in the wide world, hunting for the sword. Perhaps they had already found it.

Then, just as she began to stand to go inside, a pair of gloved hands locked around her face, smothering her cry for help.

13

✺ ✺ ✺ ✺ ✺ ✺ ✺ ✺ ✺

Reaching the Crossroads

Mel woke to the song of the birds in the trees, and opened his eyes blearily. Fog hung heavy in the woods, and a dusting of frost coated his blanket. It was quite cold—the fire had died down in the night, and now remained a pile of smoldering embers.

He heard Misty stirring in the tent, then heard her soft footsteps a little later, followed by her surprised and inquisitive voice. "Who are you?"

"Good morning to you too," came Dusty's voice from the edge of the woods. She entered the camp, carrying three decent-sized trout. "My name is Dusty. What is your name?"

"I'm Misty. That's my brother," Misty said importantly, pointing at Mel. She cocked her head to the side, thinking. "Dust-y. Mist-y. They rhyme!"

"So they do," Dusty said with a slight smile. She crouched by the fire, prodding the coals back to life. Mel sat up and stretched. Dandio's bed was empty, Rygal was still asleep, and there was no sign of Glentree.

The Wildkid's unexpected arrival last night replaced sleep with questions in his mind, and he looked at Dusty curiously. "How did you get here? You said you'd tell us in the morning."

"I will," Dusty promised patiently. "Help me find more tinder for the fire."

126

Mel picked up his bedroll and blankets and went to the edge of the woods, gathering twigs, dry leaves, and moss as Rygal had directed him before. By the time he returned to the fire, Glentree and Dandio had returned, and Rygal had woken up.

Dandio and Glentree were talking to each other, and Mel only caught the end of the conversation. "We might want to go through the Flats after all, Dandio," Glentree was saying in a lowered tone. "From what Dusty's said, the need to get the sword back to Jan is even more urgent than before."

"I know," Dandio said quietly. "I'll make the decision today." He smiled to Mel. "Good morning. Got plenty of kindling, I see."

"Yep," Mel said triumphantly.

"Well, you may want to gather a little extra. The forest will thin out as we go north, and it will be harder to find wood for the fire."

Dusty stoked the fire, then spitted the trout on green branches above the flames. "There's a creek in the valley," she told Dandio. "I think it may be the last place to get clean water before we cross the border and reach Elimar."

Dandio nodded. "Very well. We need to fill up the water flasks before we leave." He sat down beside the fire.

Glentree grinned at Dusty. "Still can't believe you turned up after all this time, princess. It's very good to see you."

"You as well, Glentree," Dusty said, smiling warmly at her old comrade. "It's good to see all of you again. Sounds like some of us have been busy since we last met, too," she added, glancing at Rygal. "You took down Safacon, then? Just like Jan told us?"

"Yep." Rygal put his hands behind his head and leaned back. "We stopped him, and his Objects of Power. But we would have appreciated help," he added, grinning at Dusty.

"Well, I wish I could have. But the Mara-N'Tell has had problems of our own, unfortunately." Dusty's voice was grim. "The Jenna have grown restless. They fought the Daffodalion Army around the same time that you fought Safacon—tried to cross the Strait and invade. It was a hard conflict. They've been pushed back, but I doubt they have been defeated."

Dandio looked at her with interest. "We received reports about that—the War of the Strait. Did the Wildkids fight then, too?"

"We did not fight with the Daffonic army—they don't trust us. But the Jenna came for Kasabren, too, and then we had to fight," Dusty said. She rubbed the thin scar on her chin as she said it. "Our counter attack was successful, thankfully."

Misty, who had been feeding the animals, walked over again. "What's Mara-Nin-tell?" she asked.

Dusty smiled at her. "Mara-N'Tell," she corrected. "It is my tribe—*Mara* is our word for clan. N'Tell means…" she thought for a moment, brow furrowed slightly. "I can't remember the word in Coonsian—it's an animal, a fierce one…"

"Wolf? Bear?" Mel suggested helpfully.

"No…" Dusty sounded irritated at herself.

"Lion," Rygal said, sitting up as he remembered.

"Yes, lion," Dusty said, nodding.

Rygal stared at her and shook his head slowly. "I still can't believe you're here," he said. "How *did* you get here, anyway?"

Dusty leaned away from the fire, watching the fish cook as the other companions grouped around. "My people have heard rumors. The Darkness is stirring. From what Dandio told me last night, it sounds like it's coming after the sword, sending the serpentines after it." She looked at Mel.

"The Darkness was tracking me," Mel said. Again, he felt the familiar pang of guilt. The Darkness had indeed been tracking him—and it had nearly killed him. But Llyrion had been there to save him.

Dusty nodded slowly. "What I don't understand is why Terrax wants the sword at all. He knows he can't wield it. So why waste strength and soldiers pursuing you?"

"I might have a clue to that question," Dandio said, and they all looked at him. "I've been thinking about it for a few days now. If all Terrax intended was to cause chaos by stealing the sword, he's succeeded. And I think by now we can confirm that he does not want the sword to wield it—because if he did, he would have simply kept it for himself, not sell it to the peddler in Appledale. So… why come after us again in the North Gully?" He glanced around the circle, waiting for someone to guess.

Rygal raised his hand slowly, almost like he was in school. "He doesn't want the sword as a weapon… he wants it for something else, something he only learned about later?" he guessed hesitantly.

"Exactly," Dandio said, smiling. "What do we know about Terrax, Misty?"

Misty looked up, her brow furrowed. "He's an Elven outlaw, and he's descended from Liridox," she stated.

"Descended from Liridox," Dandio echoed, nodding. "Now, here's my theory. Liridox's legacy, the great kingdom of Elvengate, ultimately came to ruin due to the Dividing War. Liridox himself was killed in that battle, yet to this day, his descendants blame the ruin of Elvengate on one factor. Does anyone know what that is?"

There was an uncertain pause before Glentree spoke unexpectedly. "The Star-Stones," he said slowly. "The Star king gifted a Stone to each of the three rulers—Liridox believed himself slighted."

"Yes. Yes." Dandio nodded rapidly. "Liridox wanted to use the Stones to gain greater power, something forbidden by the Star king. So Elvengate did not receive a Stone. When the Dividing War came, Elvengate fell, and the people of Liridox still believe that they could have saved their kingdom if they'd had a Star-Stone."

Mel frowned. The pieces were beginning to come together in his mind, but he couldn't quite place it. Then, in another moment, he understood. "Wait… the stone in Drisilas' hilt… it's a Star-Stone, right? So that's why Terrax…"

"That's why Terrax wants the sword," Dandio finished as Mel trailed off. The others looked thoughtful. "It's still just a theory," Dandio added, "but the more I think about it, the more plausible I find it. At first, Terrax was hired to merely steal the sword, but now he has likely learned about its true powers—that's what he was referring to before the fight in the North Gully. Now, he wants the stone of Drisilas—it would be the greatest asset to the Elven kingdom he hopes to rebuild."

There was a brief pause. Dandio stood. "Just something to think about as we walk. Let's eat breakfast, and then get going. We should hopefully reach the edge of the Flats today."

There was that word again—the Flats. Mel wondered what he was talking about.

After eating, they packed up camp, loaded the gear on the pack pony, and started north. As Dandio had predicted, the trees began to thin out, the dense underbrush slowly fading away into wiry bushes and clumps of grass. The white sky shone through the boughs of the trees, growing brighter as they walked.

Around evening, they reached the crossroads. The road split in two; one path curved south sharply, leading towards the Elven city of Elimar. The other path continued the westward direction, but slanted north again. The north road left the forest behind, and Mel could see a wide expanse of emptiness before them.

He nudged Rygal and pointed. "What's that?"

Rygal looked up. "That's the Flats—Deadmen's Flats," he explained. "Fastest way into Caer Sia, naturally, but I'm not sure if Dandio will want to go through there."

"Why?"

"It tends to be crawling with serpentines this time of year—nesting ones. There's a chance the ones sent by the Darkness won't be there, but I'm not sure Dandio will want to risk it."

They stopped at the crossroads. "We have two choices facing us," Dandio said. "We will have to decide between time and safety, and unfortunately neither can be guaranteed entirely."

He pointed through the trees at the vast expanse of white flatland to their right. "Going straight across Deadmen's Flats will get us to Caer Sia in two days at most. That's the fastest way there as it bypasses the mountains, which saves us hiking up through the pass. But as Rygal pointed out, the serpentines sometimes congregate there, and it's their nesting time now." He pointed left, down the other road. "This route would be safer—it goes due west, and would place us near Elimar. The problem is that it's a solid four day's walk to the border from here, and another two days from Elimar to Sia."

A pause. "We'll settle this the old fashioned way," Glentree said. "A vote. We've all been on this journey together thus far, so we'll make the decision together." He hesitated, then turned to his leader. "And—if you're askin' my opinion, then I'd say we take the road through the Flats. Time is our greatest concern, and we've fought worse things than snakes."

"I agree with him," Rygal said, peering through the trees at the wasteland beyond. "Terrax could be getting closer to Caer Sia every day—and who knows what the Darkness is up to."

"Then you two both suggest we go through the Flats?" Dandio said.

"Yes—I mean, unless the serpentines in the Flats are controlled by the Darkness, they shouldn't bother us at all," Rygal said with a shrug. "We'll probably be fine."

"As I remember," Dusty cut in testily, "the last time you said that was right before we sailed the canoe over the Siren's swamp with Iriam. And you said it again when we got on the ship…"

To Dusty's credit, Rygal's confident smile faded and he flushed.

The Wildkid turned to Dandio, finishing her story about when Rygal had said *we'll probably be fine.* "Anyway, I will travel the Flats, if everyone else chooses to do so. But I would think it foolish.

I'm not sure if it's worth risking the entire mission just to save time."

"Yes," Misty agreed, nodding eagerly. "And I don't want to go through the Flats."

Mel felt all their eyes fix on him, as if his vote would change everything. He felt the weight of his decision. "I…I don't want to go through the Flats," he said slowly, his voice very small in the silence. "But I also feel that might be best, because we have to get Drisilas back to Jan. But—I don't want to decide for everyone."

Now they all turned back to Dandio. The Liznee was silent for a long moment, surveying his companions, then finally nodded. "Despite the danger, I believe we will travel through Deadmen's Flats. I feel time is more important than the potential danger—if we take too long to return the sword, we may be too late to stop Terrax at all."

A moment of silence—Mel could tell Dusty was worried, but she wasn't going to argue with Dandio.

"Now," Dandio said briskly, standing. "We'll set up camp here and rest for the night, then get an early start tomorrow and travel as quickly as we can."

They built a fire and set up the tent. Dusty scouted the area and returned with a rabbit, which they cooked in a stew. The hot meal in the chill of early evening was comforting in a strange way. The sun sank below the horizon, causing the Flats to glow silver. There was something beautiful and haunting about them. Mel felt an odd chill run through him as he looked at towards the north. There was no telling what would happen tomorrow.

Even though they had marched hard all day, Mel struggled to fall asleep. He tossed and turned in his blankets beside the fire, then finally lay on his back, looking up at the stars. He wondered if his mother, miles away, was looking up at those same stars.

He rolled over again to look at Dandio—the Liznee was seated beside the fire, staring into the flames. "Dandio…I was wondering, where did Drisilas come from? You mentioned before that it has the same magic in it as the Darkness—but wasn't it always a Liznee weapon?"

"Not the same magic, exactly," Dandio said, smiling at him. "But I can tell you. In answer to your question, no, it was not a Liznee-made blade. It is a magic far older than ours, one when the Star-King formed an alliance with the first men. As a token of their alliance, the Stars gifted the three rulers of the world with a Star-Stone— smooth blue stones, each with a different sort of power. One such stone was called Isilas, meaning 'stone of fire' in the Star-tongue, and it was filled with the power of the Fyrocrians: light and flame and strength. This stone was first given to Lord Sindian of the Liznees, but after the Dividing War, the stone was lost. It was recovered by the tribe of Lia, a tribe of hama-dryads in western Daffodalion, and they kept it safe for the next two centuries."

"What is a hama-dryad?" Misty asked curiously. She too was awake, and listening with rapt attention.

"A being that is half-human, half-dryad," Dandio replied. "As you know, the dryads are the spirits of the trees, so a hama-dryad can speak the tree-language, though they live in the outer world like men. This hama-dryad tribe was attacked one day by the Jenna, cunning warriors from the far east. The Jenna destroyed much of their village. The princess of the tribe, a young woman named Nihm-Lia, managed to escape with her father the chieftain and her infant son. But she did not hide. Instead she ran northwest to Caer Sia."

Dandio paused. The light playing on his features as memories crossed his face. "I remember that day—the very day we led a garrison back into the wild to help the hama-dryads. As thanks for our help, the tribe of Lia gave Jan the long-lost Star-Stone, and when we returned victorious, he had a great sword forged, and the stone Isilas set in its hilt. And so Drisilas—which means 'sword of fire' in the Star-tongue—was made, allowing us a defense against the Darkness."

"So that's why the Darkness wants the sword?" Mel asked slowly, piecing it together.

Dandio nodded. "Drisilas alone may offer some defense against the Darkness. But its true power lies in the Star-Stone. Jan knows more about that power than I do. The sooner we return Drisilas to him, the safer Sia will be from the Darkness."

He stopped. The crickets were chirping in the low bracken, and from somewhere in the forest an owl hooted.

"What happened to Nihm?" Misty asked, eyes wide.

Dandio took a deep, heavy breath. "She was slain," he said quietly. "She led the final charge against the Jenna, and fell just before our victory. She gave everything for her people, and it was worth it, for the Lia tribe survived."

Silence fell. Mel thought of Nihm-Lia, giving her life for her people, or of Llyrion, who had died for their cause—it was strange to think of. That one could ever truly give everything. Mel wasn't sure if he could.

Rygal laid down on his mat on Mel's other side. Dandio turned back to the fire. There were soft clicks and muted conversation from Dusty and Glentree as they tended Nella and the pony.

"Rygal," Mel said, turning to face him, "what happened to Nihm-Lia's son? Did he die too?"

"Dunno," Rygal mumbled sleepily. "Stories don't say. I think he made it, maybe." With that he fell asleep.

Mel lay on his back, staring at the stars again. Sometime after moonrise, he finally drifted off to sleep.

14

∽ ∽ ∽ ∽ ∽ ∽ ∽ ∽ ∽

The Second Source

Caer Sia, the same evening

Allie regained her consciousness with a splitting headache and no idea where she was.

It was very dark and cold. There was a musty stench in the air and a dampness that bit into her skin felt vaguely familiar, but her half-conscious mind couldn't place it. Then, gradually, her memories returned, and with it, her fear.

They had met with the kragon lord. Fireclaw had said that Adderstrike and Terrax had likely both been hired by the same person—someone who wanted the sword, wanted power, and most of all, wanted to see the Liznees dead. Then she had sat on the drawbridge, deep in thought, trying to sort out all the information Fireclaw had given them. Trying to understand who could be behind it all.

And then someone had grabbed her from behind, terrifyingly strong hands gripping her and muffling her face in a sour-smelling rag, stifling her cry of alarm. She had struggled frantically for a few seconds before the drug in the rag clouded her mind, and she sank into unconsciousness.

Where was she now?

She blinked. Every muscle in her body felt weak, and her head still spun from the effects of the drug. She was in a stone room. The only light came from a weak lantern on the floor, the little flame sputtering in the damp. Her ankles were shackled and chained to the wall. Painfully, she pulled herself up to a sitting position and looked around momentarily, at a loss.

Finally, she realized where she was. This room—it was below ground, deep in the bowels of Castle Sia. It had been a prison block once, but since it was constructed directly under the river, the wetness had long ago weakened the construction and made it unfit to house prisoners. In fact, these cells had been untouched for years. Sometimes, she would hide down here, reading by the light of a lantern in peaceful solitude.

She felt anything but peaceful now—and worse, she wasn't alone.

"Glad to see you're awake, princess."

The familiar voice made her jump. Standing inside the cell, leaning against the wall, a smirk on his face, was Drona.

"Don't scream," Drona continued, his voice calm and level. "I really don't want to have to kill you. But seeing as you serve very little purpose to me, I will, if for an instant you compromise my plan."

Allie's eyes flicked to a slight movement just beside her. A burly, unfamiliar man towered above her, one hand gripping a knife, his piggy black eyes riveted on her.

"What are you doing?" she asked Drona finally, her heart pounding.

"I am doing what is in Coonsia's best interest," Drona said smoothly. "I am doing what has to be done, and what your uncle is too soft-hearted to do. Terrax nearly ruined everything with that stunt of his when he stole the sword—I told him to be more subtle, but he's dreadfully stubborn, as you might imagine."

The words hit Allie like a thunderclap. "*You?*" she said hoarsely, her stomach twisting. "*You're* the one who hired Terrax? You hired Adderstrike?"

"So I did." Drona's face soured at the name of the kragon. "Adderstrike was hard to bargain with. Quite arrogant, that one. It matters little. Once he and Terrax have served their purpose, I have no more use for them, and the Darkness can rot their bones."

Allie stared at him, unable to form words, looking in shock at the man they had trusted as an ally. The one who had seemed to be helping them. All this time... he had been the very person they had hoped to find and stop.

"Why?" she said finally. "How could you?"

Drona's face darkened. "Because I was robbed. Cheated. Years and years of faithful service to this country, to Caer Sia, and all along waiting with the expectant hope—that I would be king. Jan had yet to marry and produce an heir, so by law, Dandio's firstborn son would be king. But if a male heir was not produced, then the crown would go to... his steward."

"You," Allie whispered, slowly understanding.

Drona smiled. "You can imagine my excitement on the day you were born. A female. The possibility that I could rule was not gone yet. And then," his voice lowered, and his smile vanished, replaced by hatred, "and then, your mother, barely a week after bringing her *child* into the world, suggested that the law be changed. *Why should there be one law for men and another for women,* she said. Why should a *queen* not ascend to the throne?" Drona crouched in front of her, so close she could feel his warm breath on her face. "Your uncle agreed, naturally, and together they brought their petition to the council. And so the law… a law that had stood for centuries… was changed. For you. Just so that one day your spoiled self could sit on the throne." His face twisted; a maddened light shone in his eyes as he brought his silver dagger closer to her face. "I'd like to carve you to ribbons just to make you understand the betrayal I felt on that day."

Drona ran the knife delicately down the side of her face, sending chills down her spine. Allie shrank back, her heart pounding. Then Drona straightened.

"Of course, I still need you alive, so I will be patient. Terrax has reported that his work is almost complete. Soon, your father will return with Drisilas. And the Darkness will follow."

"They'll destroy it," Allie managed to pant. "My father and Ĵan— they'll beat the Darkness with Drisilas, and drive it back to its lair, just like they did before."

Drona smiled. "Not if Terrax has the sword. Not if someone, perhaps, slips a knife into the king's back and renders him… incapable of wielding his beloved weapon."

Allie fought hard to keep her face calm, though she was trembling. "*You* are no match for Ĵan," she spat.

Drona gave a short bark of laughter. "Of course I'm not. But Terrax is. Terrax and Adderstrike will come and fight the Red Dawn army. Then, while they are occupied in battle, the Darkness will come too. It will consume them all—Terrax, Adderstrike, Ĵan, Drisilas. And Coonsia will start afresh, a blank canvas, prepared for *me* to lead her to glory, as it should have been." He glared at Allie. "Caer Sia was the strongest military city in Orlell before Ĵan ascended the throne, did you know that? We were feared, we were great. Jan's soft heart, his weakness, has made our enemies braver. No wonder men like Terrax roam free."

"Jan has kept peace for longer than any other king before him," Allie stated bravely.

"Peace?" Drona raised his eyebrows. "Is that what he calls it now? He is weak. You are weak, and you will never be fit to rule this great city." He crouched in front of her again, fingering the knife. "The Darkness will come, and you can do nothing to stop it. Your father will arrive too late. And Jan can do nothing against the Darkness without Drisilas."

"You're wrong," Allie said, trembling. "We'll stop it, just like we'll stop you. I'm not afraid of you, Drona."

Drona studied her, and then laughed softly. "Don't lie, princess. You are terrified. You have never been good at hiding your emotions."

He straightened and nodded to the burly outlaw. "Gag her and bring her with us. We need money to repay Terrax for his service, ransom money that she will bring. After that, Adderstrike can eat her flesh for all I care."

Rough hands gripped Allie from behind, hauling her up to her feet. The chain bit painfully into her ankles, and she choked back a cry. Tears of sheer terror burned behind her vision as the guard gripped her wrists. She opened her mouth to scream, and the outlaw clamped his dirty hand over her face so hard she saw stars.

"Gently," Drona said. "No use in damaging our prize." He frowned slightly. "But then again, an opportunity like this is hard to come by. I only need you alive, after all."

The weak light glittered on the blade of his knife as he approached, a perverted sort of satisfaction in his eyes. Allie no longer trembled—she stood terrified, held in place by the guard, as the traitorous steward drew close.

"That's enough, Drona."

A familiar voice spoke from the shadows, a safe voice, a beloved voice—Allie almost sobbed with relief.

Drona whipped around.

Jan appeared in the doorway of the cell. His green eyes scanned the scene quickly before landing on his former steward. "I never thought you were the gloating type, Drona," he said, almost casually. "Or the type to spill your entire evil plot to your prisoner, without checking to be sure you were alone."

"How did you—" Drona sputtered.

Jan jerked his head to the right. "Side door. The one that leads above ground. Actually, if you hadn't been talking, you might have heard the creak of it opening." His eyes hardened. "Now, let her go, and we can talk this out reasonably."

Drona was stunned at Jan's sudden appearance. But he recovered quickly. "There's nothing to talk about, Jan," he spat. "You have lost. Do you think all the work I've done to ensure that the Darkness comes here will change if I surrender? It's already coming. It follows the sword, the sword that fool Dandio brings here even now. Paving the road for the Darkness, in fact." He laughed.

Jan had not moved. "Whatever you say, my order still stands. Let her go now, and save yourself the pain."

Drona looked him up and down and laughed again. "You're nothing without the sword, Jan. Even if you had Drisilas in your hands, I know you don't have it in you to kill. That's why you've sent your little brother to do all the dirty work for you again, isn't it?"

"Once more, Drona. Let her go."

"Oh, I'll let her go," Drona hissed. He seized Allie by the back of her vest with terrifying strength, pulling her close and pressing the knife against her throat. "I'll let her go after I've finished what I should have done the moment she became your heir!"

Jan moved so fast Allie barely saw it coming. He crossed the distance between him and Drona with sudden speed, both hands glowing with red energy. The guard jumped in front of him—Jan gripped him by the back of the neck and slammed his head into the wall; as the stunned outlaw reeled to the side, Jan punched him in the center of the face, making him stagger back.

But Drona reacted just as fast—he had expected the king would attack, and shoved Allie away. Allie crashed to the ground and started to stand, desperate to help in the unfolding fight. But the chain held her to the wall. Drona sprang at Jan's turned back, the knife flashing in his hand.

Jan caught his steward's wrist before the blade came down, locking him in an iron grip. Drona shouted and squirmed, his face inches from the king's. Jan was silent, his face calm, but the look in his eyes made Allie shiver. Then his hand began to glow again, red hot—Drona shrieked as the flames bit into the flesh of his wrist. The knife clattered to the floor.

For an instant Allie was sure Jan would kill him then and there, but he didn't. He shoved Drona back, sending him crashing into the wall. Drona got to his feet, clutching his blistered arm. Jan stepped towards him again, towering over his slightly built steward, the man he had trusted.

"You confuse bravery with cruelty," he informed him crisply. "And you, in fact, are neither. You're not smart enough to be cold-hearted, nor kind enough to be brave. And you've overlooked the fact," he gripped Drona's injured arm again, making him gasp in pain, "that every person who has attempted to kill one of my family has ended up dead." The cold, conversational tone in which he said this was chilling.

"Let me go," Drona wheezed. "I can help you—you need me to stop the Darkness, Jan—it's coming."

"No," Jan said shortly, gripping Drona's blistered wrist tighter. "The only thing you have done is meddle with powers far beyond your knowledge. And you are the last person I want or need to stop the Darkness. You'll await judgment here, while we deal with the problems you have caused."

He shoved him back, and Drona sank to the ground, clutching his arm. Jan turned and knelt beside Allie. "Are you all right?"

"Yes," Allie managed to gasp, still in shock from the encounter. Jan found the keys from the unconscious outlaw and unlocked her chains.

Then a shout from outside brought both their attention back to the situation. Calls of alarm came from the guards on the wall. "The renegade kragon—he's back!" Frantic voices came from above; Allie could hear the ominous snarl of the kragon outside.

The distraction was all Drona needed. He leapt to his feet and flung the dagger at Jan's turned back; Allie cried out a warning and the king stepped out of the way just in time. Drona ran, out of the cell and down the hall, then up the flight of stairs leading to ground level. No doubt Adderstrike already waited to carry him to safety.

Jan started to pursue him, then stopped, realizing there was no use pursuing him now. Allie looked up at her uncle's face. What Drona had told them was slowly sinking in.

The Darkness was coming.

"What do we do?" Allie asked softly, suddenly feeling very small and powerless. She had only heard rumors of the black wraith of death, but she understood the gravity of what was happening.

Jan set his jaw as they walked the opposite direction down the hall, to the other flight of stairs that would take them inside the palace. "With or without Drisilas, we must be ready."

"Drona's working for the Darkness," Allie stammered, stunned. "He's letting it do the work of conquering Sia for him and then he'll take over!"

Jan shook his head. "Drona is playing the ventriloquist—he has been pulling the strings of Terrax and Adderstrike this whole time. He doesn't understand the Darkness—it won't differentiate between him and us. It will consume us all if it gets the chance."

Allie swallowed. Her mouth was dry with fear as they entered the palace. She heard the distinctive low thrum of the kragon's wings, and heard the muffled confusion of the guards as Adderstrike left. Carrying Drona to safety before the Darkness came to destroy everything.

"So what should we do?" she asked again, her heart pounding.

Jan glanced outside. A cold resolve shone in his green eyes. "We will fight. We must hold it off for however long it takes for Dandio to come with the sword." He paused, and finished under his breath. "And we'll hope he gets here fast."

PART 2

The Shadow

15

∽ ∽ ∽ ∽ ∽ ∽ ∽ ∽ ∽

Deadmen's Flats

Glentree woke them at dawn. They ate a meager breakfast, then loaded the gear onto the pack pony so that Nella could walk freely. Mel guessed that if they ran into trouble, they would need Nella to help fight.

"We'll head due north west," Glentree was saying as he etched out a rough map in the dirt. "Once we're through the Flats, we'll only have to head west across the border." He straightened and brushed the dust off his knees.

"Come on, we'd better get going," said Rygal, squinting at the sun, which was rising in height and in heat. Dandio stood at the far edge of the clearing, studying the white expanse, deep in thought. He turned at Rygal's voice and nodded.

"Right then. Glentree, you lead. I'll take the rear."

He caught Dusty's arm and spoke quietly to her—Mel had stopped to tie his shoe, and so he heard every word. "Keep the children close. If we are attacked, get them on Nella and take the sword to Elimar." Dusty nodded wordlessly and fell into place behind Rygal.

"Stay close," Dandio told Mel and Misty as they followed Dusty. The Liznee brought up the rear of the party, his hand resting on his sword hilt, his green eyes scanning the terrain.

In a few minutes, they had left the forest behind and started out

149

across the Flats. Deadmen's Flats, Mel thought, had been accurately named. There was no vegetation growing aside from a few spindly bushes. A crow cawed periodically in the distance, and a few small lizards scampered back and forth between stones.

The whole place was wide and gray, with ridges of hulking, crumbling boulders rising up from the ground. To Mel, the rock ridges looked like the spine of a great beast. The path wound steadily northwest, in and out of the shadows of the rocks. The ground, Mel noticed curiously, seemed to be covered with fine white sand.

"What happened here?" he asked finally, both fascinated and chilled by the deadness of the area.

"No one really knows," Dandio told him. "These Flats might be the ruin of some great ancient lake. But they're salt flats, interestingly enough."

"Salt?" Misty repeated curiously, peering at the ground.

"Yes," Dandio said, smiling. "Anyway, we don't know why these particular salt flats are here. It's not the handiwork of the rebel Netrocrians, though. While this is an odd place, it is still a natural part of the world, just as the mountains are."

They continued on through the desolate land. Mel kept turning Dandio's words to Dusty over and over in his mind. If they were attacked, he and Misty would be loaded up and rushed to Elimar. That would lower the number of companions that could fight to three—which meant they would probably be outnumbered. Mel hated the idea of leaving them, hated the idea of fleeing helplessly into the wilds. So far, all he had done on this quest was get in the way.

On and on they went. It was around midday when the land sloped down slightly and they entered a channel, surrounded by huge white boulders. The rocks rose high above them on either side, casting large shadows on the path that contrasted the white glare from the sun. Despite the chill, Mel welcomed the shade. With the constant exercise, he was already damp with sweat.

"It's so quiet," Dusty said at length, her ears perked up. "Where are the serpentines?"

"Might be on the other side of the Flats," Glentree said hopefully. "We would have seen some by now, if they were out here."

"Maybe," Dandio said slowly, "but I'm not convinced that they aren't here. There are no nests that we have seen, but they might still be in the area."

Rygal sat down on a rock. "Blast these stones," he muttered crossly, removing his boot and emptying a handful of pebbles on the ground.

Mel's shoes had picked up a few rocks on the way too—he sat down and copied Rygal. As he did, he noticed something on the ground. It was about three inches long, curved slightly, coming to a point at the tip. There seemed to be something dark dried on it.

A tooth, perhaps.

At the same time, Dandio, whose mind was sharpened by years of experience, suddenly realized something had changed. For a moment he couldn't place it, then he realized that the crow, which had been cawing every few seconds, was silent. Nella's ears perked up suddenly, and she gave a low, uneasy growl.

"Something's wrong," Dandio said.

The warning came too late.

It happened so fast Mel barely had time to turn his head—he

heard a hissing snarl followed by a scraping sound as something crept out from behind the boulders; out of the corner of his eye he saw a flash of green scales and bat like wings.

Misty screamed as the beast lumbered forward—Mel whirled around and stared. A serpentine, its curved white fangs glinting in the sunlight, opened its mouth to let out a horrible hissing scream of fury. It seemed to be the same one that had attacked them in Appledale—Mel could see scars left on its scales from Rygal's sword.

"Back!" Dandio barked, drawing his sword and stepping toward the creature. The serpentine turned slowly, studying the Liznee, its forked tongue lashing in and out through its jaws. Then it spoke. Its voice was hollow and echoing.

"I have sent this servant to fetch the sword. This loyal servant will give you one chance to hand over the blade, or it will destroy all of you. This is your only choice. Do you understand, Liznee? Surely you understand my power."

Dandio had stopped in his tracks at the beast's voice. Mel could only stare, dumbfounded. He knew the serpentines couldn't communicate on their own…which meant the Darkness itself was speaking through it.

Like it had in Appledale.

Chills ran down his spine, both from the terror of the memory, and from the fact that battle was about to begin.

"Go back to your master," Dandio said, his voice level. "Go back and tell it that we are not going to accept these terms. The sword will be its downfall."

The serpentine hissed menacingly and lunged.

Dandio slashed at it as it moved, dodging out of the way. Rygal and Glentree charged forward to join him. Mel hesitated beside the boulders, not sure what to do, and looked over at Dusty—

Who, he realized with a jolt, wasn't obeying Dandio's order to retreat, but instead had crouched behind a rock and had set an arrow to the string of her bow. As the serpentine's tail whipped across Rygal's chest and sent him stumbling back, Dusty loosed the arrow, sending it plunging into the creature's mouth.

The serpentine let out another horrible scream, this time in pain, and reeled back. Dusty drew out another arrow and shot again; the arrow glanced over the creature's wing. The serpentine turned very slowly, its bulbous white eyes fixing on Dusty and the two children beside her.

"Go!" Dusty shouted, pushing Mel and Misty away as the serpentine wrenched the arrow free and charged at her. She loosed a third shot at the creature, missed, and turned to flee. Mel's heart plummeted in fear as the serpentine spread its wings and bounded after her. But there was no way she could outrun it, it had nearly caught her.

"Dusty!" Misty cried in fear.

Then a blast of crackling red struck the serpentine in the shoulder and flung it sideways, away from the Wildkid. "Keep going!" Dandio ordered, and the other companions ran down the trail through the channel of towering gray rocks. Mel trailed behind, unable to tear his eyes away from the scene. Dandio stepped forward, his hands glowing red, watching as the serpentine turned to him. Blood trailed from its mouth and wing, but it paid the wounds no heed as it snarled defiantly at Dandio, ready to fight to the end.

It charged forward, spreading its wings mid-leap, avoiding the second blast that Dandio shot at its feet, and soared through the air at the Liznee. Dandio dove out of its grasp as it came down clawing and screaming in fury. Nella leapt between the beast and her master, her teeth bared and her claws slashing. The serpentine stumbled under the brunt of the young gryphon's attack, but it recovered quickly, and snapped its long fangs at Nella's paws. The young gryphon snarled back, but now the serpentine's eyes had fixed on the sword strapped to Nella's saddlebags.

Drisilas' stone glinted, reflected in the white eyes of the serpentine. It pounced on the gryphon, its teeth tearing at the leather straps that held the sword. Nella gave a snarl of fury and squirmed, but the serpentine held fast, ripping Drisilas free.

"Hey!" Mel shouted, and charged forward, shoving the serpentine in the shoulder with both hands. Off balance, the beast fell awkwardly from Nella's back. Mel scooped up the sword and ran down the rocky channel, his eyes on the forms of his other companions.

The serpentine gave a furious scream that made Mel's teeth rattle—he gripped the sword, running for all he was worth. In a split second of memory, he was in the North Gully caves again, fleeing the danger, running from the Dwarves. Except this was much worse.

"Come on, Mel!" he heard Rygal shout ahead. Ignoring Dandio's order to retreat, both Glentree and Rygal had turned back, running to Mel's aid. The same moment he had the thought, a dark shadow settled over him from above, and the serpentine caught him with a swirl of bat-like wings.

Mel tried to turn to face it, but before he could, the creature seized him by the shoulders and flung him face down. Mel crashed to the ground, landing painfully on his chest on the hard rocks. Before he could get up again, the serpentine pounced on top of him, its rancid breath warm on the back of his neck, its claws digging into his skin; Mel had the sudden, shocking realization that he was about to die.

Then a sudden explosion of red fire came from above and knocked the serpentine off him. Dandio had reached them, and now squared off with the attacker again. The serpentine hissed and lunged; Dandio leapt back out of the way, and gripping Mel's arm, led him off the trail as the serpentine pursued them. Mel clutched Drisilas to his chest, his whole body trembling.

Dandio fired another blast at the serpentine, and it paused, hissing. Mel looked around wildly; they were trapped in a narrow alcove that split off of the main road. Rock wall surrounded them on all sides. The serpentine had them backed into a dead end.

"Stay back!" Dandio warned. Mel shrank against the wall, his mouth dry with terror. Dandio stood between Mel and the hissing creature, red light crackling in his fists, his green eyes fixed on the monster before them. The serpentine sized him up, its chest vibrating with the strange hissing snarl. Then it lunged forward, pinning Dandio to the ground on his back before he could dodge. Its teeth flashed as it struck—Dandio gripped its muzzle in both hands, forcing the teeth away from his throat, and instead the creature's fangs sank into his shoulder.

"Dandio!" Glentree shouted. Mel caught glimpses of his other companions as they ran back down the path toward the battle.

The serpentine hissed and pulled free—Dandio adjusted his grip and locked both arms around the serpentine's wings, holding it down. The creature howled in fury, squirming wildly, fighting the Liznee's strength with all of its own. Mel flinched back, trapped against the rocks. Any second now, the creature would break free, and then it would all be over.

But Dandio didn't let go. Mel saw the monster's teeth flash as it struck at the Liznee again and again, worsening the wound on Dandio's shoulder, but still his grip stayed tight even as his blood streaked the ground.

Then, abruptly, the serpentine reared back its head, jaws wide open, preparing to bite the Liznee's head clean off. In the second it lunged down, Dandio let go and shoved his right hand up into the serpentine's throat.

There was a blast of red, a hissing shriek quickly cut off, and the snake slumped over on top of the still figure under it.

Glentree reached them first, shoving the serpentine's mangled body off of Dandio. Mel fell to his knees, his legs feeling like jelly, watching in numb silence as Glentree knelt beside the Liznee. "Dandio? Dandio, can you hear me? Hang on—hold on…"

Dandio's face was deathly pale and drawn with pain. He was still conscious, breathing heavily. Blood wet the ground around him from the wound in his shoulder, and his right arm was slashed and covered in the serpentine's spit and blood.

"Dandio…" Mel mumbled, as cold despair seeped into his very core. The other companions arrived, out of breath, and stood back in shocked silence.

Glentree sat up abruptly. "Dusty, get the medical kit an' bring it here. We've got to have an antidote of some kind in there. Rygal, I'll need your help to get him on the pony."

"How… is there… will he…" Rygal started, his face almost as pale as Dandio's, looking absolutely at a loss.

Glentree's normally cheery face was pallid and drawn with fear. "I don't know. But he's not gone yet. Now we have to hurry," he said shortly.

Dusty handed him the medicine kit, then unloaded the gear from the pony's back and placed it on Nella. Misty stood beside the gryphon—she was crying softly but seemed to be unhurt.

Mel finally managed to stand and moved towards Dandio, his whole body trembling. The Liznee was still breathing, he could see, but the breaths sounded painfully labored. A memory of Llyrion, laying still and gasping for breath, came unbidden into Mel's mind, and tears stung behind his eyes.

Glentree cleaned the wound in Dandio's shoulder with the water from one of the flasks, all the while murmuring under his breath. "Come on Cap'n… don't give out on me now… you'll be all right, it'll be all right…" His fervent whispering was the only indication of the fear that filled his mind.

Glentree applied an antiseptic balm to the wound before bandaging it; Dandio gave a low murmur of pain, then fell back again, half conscious. Glentree and Rygal managed, very slowly and carefully, to lift the Liznee's still form and set him on the pony's back. Glentree said that it would be best if he stayed in a sitting position, so Dusty sat up behind him, holding the limp body upright.

"We'll get out of the Flats and rest for a while," Glentree told them, and turned back to the trail.

They continued moving forward. Glentree barely allowed them to rest; the lingering threat of serpentines made escaping the Flats crucial. Mel felt too tired and fearful to think of anything beyond taking one step at a time, one foot in front of the other. Misty looked just as tired, but she adamantly refused to let Mel carry her.

Stars twinkled brightly overhead by the time they finally reached the edge of the Flats. They set up camp, and Dusty built a small fire.

Mel lay in silence, watching the crackling flames. The recent horror of the battle made him unable to process much else. Sometime around midnight, it registered, for the first time, that Dandio might die. His hero, dying for him—the thought sent a jolt of cold grief through his chest, and he huddled in the dark as silent tears rolled down his face.

Then another emotion—stronger than the grief and fear—rose inside of him. A raw determination, like the look he had seen in Dandio's eyes even as the serpentine had attacked him. Dandio had saved his life. Mel knew without a hint of doubt that he could not let that go to waste. He also knew, in the same moment, that if Dandio died, something inside him would break.

"That's not going to happen," he choked hoarsely to himself, and looked over at the Liznee's still form. "I'm not going to let you die, Dandio—I promise."

Whatever he could do to fulfill that promise, whatever could be done, Mel was prepared. He did know, at least, that if they hurried, they might reach Caer Sia in time to save him.

16

Reaching the Border

Mel's feet felt like lead. Rygal had roused them at dawn and they had been walking all day, pausing only for a quick bite of food and a little rest. They finally stopped a little after midday for an hour's rest. He slumped painfully to the ground, his legs protesting as he sat. Misty sat down on one of the packs. Dirt streaked her face, and her blonde hair was matted. She looked exhausted, and Mel knew how she felt.

Dusty handed out some dried meat and bread. Mel took his but didn't eat it. He felt too tired to eat, too tired to drink, too tired to do anything except lay down and sleep for a long, long time. But then he glanced over at the still figure laying under the blanket, and his weariness drained away.

In the past twenty-four hours, Dandio hadn't improved. The bleeding had finally stopped, but the wound had swollen, the skin around it an unnatural orange-colored hue. The symptoms of the serpentine's poison had begun to show, and Dandio's brow burned with fever. For a few hours last night Dandio had tossed and turned, muttering names and places Mel had never heard of. But now he was still again, barely breathing. There was no antidote in the medical kit that could combat the serpentine's venom; the best they could do was wash the wound and try to keep Dandio comfortable.

Mel wrapped his cloak around himself. At least they were out of the Flats now, and back in the forest. Glentree estimated they were about ten miles from the border between Coonsia and Daffodalion. Mel had never been to Coonsia, or Caer Sia, for that matter. He would have felt more excited at the prospect of seeing such a city, had the circumstances not been so urgent.

Glentree came and sat down heavily beside the fire across from Mel. Lines of worry were etched around his tired eyes. "Mel," he said unexpectedly, and Mel looked up at him. "There's somethin' I've been meaning to speak to you about. Both of you," he added, nodding to Misty.

"What is it?" Mel asked, hearing the seriousness in his voice.

Glentree continued. "Quests are always difficult," he said. "We all knew this, and by now, you and Misty know that too. But this venture, it's even more dangerous now that we know the Darkness is in the game." He paused before continuing. "Dandio'd do anything to keep you two safe. He meant to tell you this before, but…" he nodded to the still figure in the tent. Mel felt a familiar stab of guilt. "There's no telling what we'll face in Caer Sia, but we're only about twenty miles north from Elimar. Dusty has already agreed to take you two there if you choose. Then you can get a carriage back to Appledale."

Back to Appledale. The words echoed again and again in Mel's mind. His heart leaped. Back to Appledale. Back to his home, his friends, and his family—his family. "But…would we be safe there?" he managed to ask.

"We believe so," Glentree said. "Both the North Gully encounter and the serpentine attack yesterday showed us that the Darkness has picked up our trail again, so I think that's a good sign that its eyes are no longer on Appledale."

Mel leaned back against the packs, thinking, hope filling him. They could go back to Appledale, to safety and peace and normal life again. They would be able to tell all that they had done, and…

His joy turned cold.

This would be how the story would end, abandoning his companions—people who had saved his and Misty's lives over and over again—in the wilderness. What was worse, he would never know if they made it to Caer Sia or not, not for months at least, until the news circulated across the border again.

In a moment, he knew there was no way he could do that. They had all fought for this cause. Llyrion had died for it. Dandio had saved Mel's life, possibly at the cost of his own.

And ultimately, Mel had found the sword. Somehow, he felt bound to see this quest through.

Misty spoke slowly, her sweet voice so very different from Glentree's hoarse and tired one. "I want to go home," she said. "But if Dusty takes us there, then that only leaves you and Rygal to protect Dandio and the sword." She thought for a moment, then added dreamily, "Besides, I've never been to Caer Sia, and it sounds lovely."

Mel had to smile in admiration at his brave little sister. He looked at Glentree. "She's right. We'll go if you ask us to—but I owe Dandio my life. We can't just leave you all here."

Glentree gave them both a tired but proud smile. "Good to 'ear it. Well, why don't you two get a little more rest—we'll get going again in a few minutes."

Mel ate the food Dusty had given him and settled back against the packs. Across the camp, Dandio stirred and muttered something in his sleep. Rygal crossed quickly to him, and Mel looked up at Glentree worriedly.

"Glentree...do you think he'll make it?"

Glentree doused the fire as he thought. "I don't know, Mel," he admitted finally. "He's lost a lot of blood, and the venom's started to affect him. But he's strong, Mel—and he's stubborn." He smiled faintly. "He's survived a lot worse than this before, and I think if we get to Sia in time... he just might make it."

Rygal had knelt beside Dandio and was gently examining him, then stood and moved to Glentree. "He's in bad shape, Glentree— his forehead's burning up."

Glentree nodded, standing. "Let's get going again. Dusty, bring the pony over."

The path led northwest, over the Hallas River, and the old bridge that spanned the gray waters. Once past the river, the trees grew denser, tall firs and hemlocks. Glentree led them on.

"Might be able to make it if we keep up this pace," the big man said optimistically, fingering the pony's reins. They had fastened a makeshift stretcher for Dandio that morning and tied it to the pony's broad back, while Nella carried the gear. This meant all five of them could be on the ground. Mel figured this was best in case they ran into danger again.

He looked up at Rygal, who was walking beside him. "Rygal, I was wondering something. If it *was* the Darkness—" even the name made him shiver—"that killed Llyrion, then why didn't it just come after us then and take the sword? It probably could have beaten us."

Rygal thought about this for a moment. "I'm not sure. But I've been wondering that too. If the Darkness is half as powerful as we've been told, it could have destroyed us all and taken the sword."

"Then why didn't it?" Mel asked. He had been wondering this for a while now. Yes, the serpentines had come after them, and yes, it was clear the Darkness was pursuing them as well…but why wait to attack?

It was Glentree who spoke, very quietly, from the front of the group. "We haven't explained that to you very well. I'll do my best. The Darkness is tracking the sword—Drisilas and the Star-Stone in its hilt are leading it to Caer Sia. The Darkness doesn't have a mind or any way to track us, aside from following the Star-Stone's trace. It'll follow our trail to get into Caer Sia."

"But couldn't it have just taken the sword and used it to do that itself?" Mel asked, still puzzled.

"No, not really. Remember how Dandio explained the fire and Netrocrians—the Darkness can't touch Drisilas. Can't wield it, can't be too near it even, which is probably why it didn't attack us all the day Llyrion died." Mel remembered the Stone's powers shielding him from the Darkness in the caverns, and understood what this meant. Glentree paused. "Once the Darkness gets into Sia, it'll draw power from the destruction it causes, enough power to destroy the sword. Just like it tried to do last time."

The last sentence made them all look at him.

"Last time?" Dusty repeated, dumbfounded. "What do you mean?"

Glentree glanced at Dandio's still form, then at the four eager faces looking at him. "I…well, I don't know if it's my place to be telling ya. But…seeing as things are as they are…"

"Was the Darkness…did it attack Sia?" Mel asked. He remembered Dandio mentioning something about that, when they had camped in Elvengate. And he remembered the way the Liznee had hesitated to say any more.

Glentree took a breath. "Aye. It did. Killed 'undreds of people—Liznees and humans. And the queen mother."

Mel looked at Dandio, stunned, then back at Glentree. "It—it killed his mother?"

"Her and a whole lot more." Glentree hesitated. "Yeh see—there was a big ceremony planned. Jan's coronation, actually. They finished the ceremony, all these people in the castle celebrating—and the Darkness attacked."

His face was gray with the memories. "It killed so many—bodies everywhere, their chests frozen solid. Jan got Dandio's wife out safe, but they couldn't find Dandio. None of us could. We thought he was dead. We found him two days later, under a heap of rubble, the queen mother's body beside him. She saved him—the Darkness shot at them both, it seemed, and she took the blast for him. Most of it, anyway…a bit of the blast hit him. An' that's how he got his scar." Glentree made a sweeping motion down the right side of his face.

The others were silent, stunned by the story.

"Why…why hasn't he told us this?" Rygal asked finally, his voice soft.

Glentree sighed heavily. "He 'asn't talked about it in years. That's why they went after the Darkness shortly after that attack, though, once they got Drisilas. Jan and Dandio, trying to avenge the fallen. An' that's the last time anyone saw it." He looked at them. "You'll understand why it was so hard for Dandio to accept that it was back."

Silence fell again. Mel remembered the way Dandio had avoided dwelling on discussion about the Darkness—Mel had been skeptical then, confused of what could possibly have Dandio Ki that concerned. Now he knew, and sorrow for what the Liznee had experienced settled heavy in his stomach.

"I don't know if he'll mind you knowing or not," Glentree said, "but I know he doesn't like it being mentioned. So… keep it on the down low, all right?"

The other four nodded silently. Glentree turned down the path, taking the reins and urging the pony forward again.

· · · · · ·

They walked in silence after Glentree's story. The truth behind it seemed to have renewed Mel's determination to complete their mission.

The path widened considerably. The trees were bushy and dense, their large boughs hanging over into the road. The branches of the larger trees were almost as big around as Mel was. The early evening sun lit the trees and path, bathing the scenery in peaceful light.

Then Glentree stopped and turned. His face was completely

casual as he announced in a low voice, "Rygal, there's a figure in the shadows of the trees over there. Don't look, lad!" he added quietly as Mel started to turn.

Rygal nodded, also feigning calm. "Where?"

Glentree scratched his bald head, subtly pointing his little finger to the right as he did. "He's lying flat on the big branch partway up the cedar tree with the red bark, 'bout ten or twenty paces off."

Dusty looked over, then made a show of looking up at the sky. "He looks about your height, Rygal. He has a bow and about thirteen or fourteen arrows," she said with the tone of one commenting on the weather.

Mel forced himself not to look. The figure, whatever it was, still believed it had the element of surprise on its side, and Mel would not ruin that by staring.

Rygal jerked his head at the pony, with Dandio lying prone on the stretcher. "Cover him up with a cloak or something, Glentree. With any luck, it'll think he's luggage," he said quietly.

Dusty looked at him in exasperation as Glentree moved to do so. "Dandio, luggage? Are you serious?"

Rygal crossed his arms and spoke like he was reprimanding her, though his words were different. "You need to get Mel and Misty out of here on Nella. Go to Elimar, then to Sia and return the sword."

"No," Mel said softly, stepping between them. "Rygal, I'm done running. This time I'm going to fight. Even if I get killed, I'll at least make enough distraction for Dusty and Misty to escape with the sword. Please."

Rygal looked surprised, but he nodded. "Well—all right."

"I want to fight too," Misty said, although the very idea made her quiver with fear.

"No, Misty," Mel told her gently. He knew he couldn't allow his little sister to risk her life fighting—she had to be kept safe. He realized, suddenly, that if he died, this was the last moment they would have together. Not that it would do any good to point that out to her, he thought; he swallowed down the lump in his throat and forced a smile. "It's going to be all right. You go with Dusty now, okay?"

Dusty took her hand and led her towards the gryphon, prepared to flee if the stranger was a threat.

Rygal moved next to Mel. "Have you done any fencing or anything like that?"

"A little," Mel said. One of his friends enjoyed fencing, and Mel had sometimes sparred with him using wooden swords.

"Good—take this." Rygal handed him a long dagger. The blade felt foreign in Mel's hand, awkward and clumsy. "Aim for vital organs— lungs are good targets if you can hit them. If not, anywhere in the abdominal area will hurt."

Mel nodded, his mouth dry. He could see the stranger now, stretched out flat on the branch ahead, about five feet from the ground. He appeared to be relaxing, but the soft glint of the arrow on the string told Mel otherwise.

Glentree turned and called into the trees. "Show yourself! We can see you and are prepared to fight you if you are a foe. Answer!"

The voice that replied was not an orc's snarl, but a fair voice, somewhat like Dandio's. There was a hint of amusement there. "Whether or not I am a foe depends on whom you serve. At any rate these are my lands, and it is I who should be asking the questions."

"We are only passing through," Glentree said, keeping his voice calm. "We are headed north. As for whom we serve, we serve the High Light, and as for mortal ruler, Jan High King of Coonsia."

"Then I am not your foe in those respects," the stranger said. There was a quick movement as he slid off the branch to lean against the tree trunk. Most of his frame remained shadowed in the trees, but Mel could see the outline of a longbow held loosely in his hand. "I do not trust you, not yet. A strange group you appear. How many are you?"

"Six of us," Rygal answered. "We…are led by a Liznee." He hesitated— he had said it in hopes of scaring off the attacker; no one would want to fight a skilled Liznee warrior, after all. Now he looked uncertain.

"A Liznee?" the stranger responded, then added curiously, "Not Dandio Ki?

Rygal's sword flashed as he drew it. "You DARE speak of Dandio?!" he shouted, his voice torn in anguish. Glentree stepped forward and gripped his shoulder, pulling him back. Rygal stopped, and his head dropped wearily to his chest. His voice was heavy. "Dandio is stricken and lies dying as we speak."

"Dandio is stricken?" the voice repeated, and there was a note of dismay in the words. "That is grave news."

"Why does it matter to you?" Glentree asked cautiously. "Who are you?"

There was a pause. Then the figure stepped forward into the light. His skin was a pale blue, and his hair was silver-blond, marking him as a hama-dryad. His face was young, and he appeared to be a few years older than Rygal. His clothes were simple, woven from gray wool, and a quiver of arrows was slung at his side.

"You ask why I care?" he said quietly. "I say only this. Nihm-Lia was my mother."

17

The Tribe of Lia

The companions stared at the stranger, who moved forward slowly. He had lowered his bow, but still seemed cautious.

Glentree spoke, his voice a low rumble. "Your mother…I knew her, briefly. She's the one who saved your tribe—she ran for help."

"The Liznees saved us," the hama-dryad said quietly, looking carefully at the big man. "I was very young, so I remember little of that day. But the story…it has been the very vein of hope that runs through my people to this day. The story of how the Liznees came to our aid…and how we have yet to repay them."

"Who are you, then?" Glentree asked, lowering his weapon.

"I am Kalos-Lia. Warrior of the tribe of Lia," the hama-dryad said, bowing slightly. "And you?"

"Glentree, warrior of Sia. With me is Rygal of Gayrile, a warrior of the north, and Dusty, a Wildkid princess," Glentree said. "Dandio was leading us—he was injured on the Flats."

"The Flats?" Kalos-Lia's brow wrinkled slightly, uncertain. "No warriors have been on the Flats, no enemy that we have seen," he said, sounding suspicious.

"It was a serpentine," Rygal said from behind Glentree. "Sent by the Darkness itself."

The hama-dryad's face clouded with fear at the name. "The Darkness... but it was defeated. Or so we heard..."

"It's back, as it were," Glentree said heavily. There was a pause. Glentree looked at the hama-dryad before him. "We've nothing to offer you, understand. But I'll appeal to your tribe's debt with the Liznees. Do you know of any place where we can get treatment for him? We don't have anythin' that can treat serpentine venom."

Kalos thought a moment, then nodded. "Yes. Yes, you had best come quickly."

He turned, nodding for them to follow him off the path and into the trees. The companions followed slowly, Glentree leading the pony into the brush. Mel took Misty's hand, and she looked up at him, puzzled.

"Are we safe?"

"I'm not sure...but I think so," Mel told her slowly. Kalos-Lia had shown the same wariness around the newcomers as the Dwarve farmers had back in Tackert Fief. He wasn't going to kill them, Mel was fairly sure of that. He was still a stranger though, and Mel didn't entirely trust him. But they didn't have much of a choice. If there was any chance of saving Dandio, it would lie in the hands of the hama-dryads.

He tripped over a trailing vine—the woods were growing denser and denser, and light was fading. The pony moved uneasily through the ferns, ears flicked back uncertainly. Nella scented the breeze, her sharp eyes scanning the woods for danger. While Mel didn't feel threatened, the forest sent chills down his spine. He was an intruder, a stranger in a place that he completely didn't belong in. The whole wood seemed to radiate life as the trees bent over them, watching them with sleepy eyes. It was a strange feeling.

"There are dryads here," Dusty said softly from behind him, as if sensing his thoughts. "They inhabit the trees, the very spirits of the wood—you can tell by the… well, the very air of the place."

She paused, not sure how to explain it, but Mel understood. "Are they…going to attack us?" he asked uneasily, looking up into the boughs of the towering evergreens all around them.

Kalos-Lia spoke from ahead. "They will not attack you, not if they see you as a friend. Should you give them reason to hate you, however, know that you would not emerge alive from these woods."

Mel took a few steps away from the tree he had been observing, deciding not to risk it.

They wove through the woods for another few minutes, moving in silence. The air filled with the damp, rich smell of a forest creek somewhere beyond. Mel noticed that the evergreens had been joined by rugged gray willow trees, growing in the moist ground of the shallow valley.

In another moment, the path turned sharply to the right, and the companions stood in a grove of willows. A stream ran through the center of the grove, carving delicately along the valley basin. Reeds and cattails grew along the edges. Among the trees, almost invisible and built from the same silver-gray willow bark that filled the grove, were many small huts with dome-like roofs.

The grove was filled with hama-dryads. A few tended to the trees, trimming away stray growths and stroking the bark as if caring for a well-loved animal. They paused to watch the companions enter with a quiet interest. Mel felt their eyes settle on them as they entered, and felt an uncomfortable stir. There was no hostility in the eyes of the people. But the companions were total and utter strangers here, mortals in a place few had ever entered.

Kalos led them to a larger hut beside the creek, sheltered by a towering, craggy willow tree. An old hama-dryad sat cross-legged in the doorway of the hut, his eyes closed as if asleep. He looked up as Kalos approached, his vivid blue eyes surveying them slowly and carefully. His long beard was silvery-white, his skin a slightly darker shade of green-gray than Kalos'. There was an ancient wisdom in his wrinkled face.

"Kalos-Lia. I see you have brought guests." His voice was deep and breathy, like the wind passing through the fir trees.

Kalos bowed slightly. "Indeed I have, grandfather. They have urgent need." He turned to the companions. "Meet you Munben-Lia, chieftain of our tribe."

Mel followed his friends' examples and bowed to the chieftain. Munben stood and nodded politely.

"The trees have reported your coming. Bring your wounded within." He beckoned them inside the hut. Mel followed, looking around the inside of the simple structure. This hut was a little larger than the others, round, with multiple small, alcove-like rooms leading off of the main room. Inside smelled pleasantly of herbs and wood smoke. Candles lit the hut with a golden glow. Inside each room was a cot, and a curtain hung across the openings allowed for privacy. The whole structure reminded Mel of a beehive.

Glentree lifted Dandio into his burly arms, and at Munben's instructions, laid him carefully on one of the cots in an alcove.

Munben moved to a small shelf in the main room and fetched a few bottles of medicine, and fresh linen bandages. "What is his injury?" he asked as he did so.

"A serpentine, sir," Glentree told him. "We traveled across the Flats yesterday, and a serpentine attacked us and bit him. It's quite a story." He paused, then continued. "We would be greatly obliged to you if you're able to heal him."

Munben moved back to Dandio, gently removing the bloodstained bandages on his shoulder. Dandio had stopped tossing, and now lay still and pale, his skin clammy with perspiration. The wound still wept blood, and the flesh around the bite was discolored. Seeing it, Mel felt a stab of fear that the Liznee was already too far gone.

Munben's brow was furrowed as he examined Dandio. "I will work quickly. Serpentine venom works fast, but I think I can still save him." He paused, then looked up with a raised eyebrow. "This Liznee… this is Dandio Ki. Who are you?"

"I'm Glentree, sir. Deputy of Sia," Glentree said. "We're… well, we're on an urgent errand."

"Indeed," Munben murmured. He thought in silence as he prepared a few more vials of medicine. "Dandio saved our tribe," he said finally. "Years ago, after my daughter…" he trailed off, pain written on his face. Mel knew he was thinking of Nymn. "We are in debt to him and his people," Munben continued at length. "I will do all I can to save him."

Glentree let out a breath, relief on his face. "Thank you, sir."

Kalos led the four companions back outside. Glentree remained inside, clearly determined to stay by his leader's side. Mel still felt uncertain, but allowed himself to hope. Kalos seemed to guess his thoughts, and smiled encouragement.

"Do not fear. My grandfather is a skilled healer, and has treated serpentine bites worse than this before." He looked at Rygal. "Shall I escort you to our guest chambers? You may wish to rest for a while."

Rygal nodded and followed. Mel took one last look back at the hospital hut, hesitating. Then he returned to the hut, listening to the low voices from within.

"We can't repay you, sir," Glentree was saying, a touch of worry in his tone.

"None needed. There is some other force at play here… something I do not understand. The trees have spoken to me—they have told me of the Dark power." Munben's voice was quiet, but Mel could hear the urgency there. He peeked around the doorway, and could see the aged healer applying medicine to Dandio's shoulder.

"The Darkness," Glentree told him heavily. The big man hesitated before continuing. "Your tribe may be in danger, sir. The Darkness is tracking us and the sword. We'd hate to lead it here."

"Indeed. Nevertheless, you must wait until he is well enough to travel," Munben said. "This wound has weakened him greatly."

"But you can treat it?" Glentree asked anxiously. "We didn't have anything to help him."

"Yes, I can treat it. Serpentine venom is potent, and acts quickly once in the body. But we have something that will act faster." There was a soft rustle—Mel saw him place the dried petals of some red flower into a bowl, and crush them into a poultice. The sweet, fresh smell reached his nose from his place in the doorway.

"*Entira Rivira*, or as you call them in the Coonsian tongue, fireflowers," Munben said. "I believe you use them occasionally in Sia?"

Mel didn't understand the significance of this, but Glentree nodded. "Yes—only sometimes. They're very rare. Thank you, sir," he repeated.

"Of course. Now tell me more about this Darkness. We have only heard whispers of its name."

Mel moved away from the door as Glentree quietly told the chieftain the story. He felt he had been eavesdropping long enough. Dandio would be all right. The sweet smell from the fireflowers reassured him, soothing his anxious thoughts as he jogged to catch up as Kalos led the companions through the little village.

......

Mel slept soundly that night, lulled to sleep by the swishing willows. The hut, though small, was quite cozy, and the three of them had spread out their bedrolls and gone to sleep fairly quickly. In the morning there was no sign of Glentree or Rygal.

"They're staying in the hut next to us," Dusty explained when Mel asked. "Glentree was up late last night speaking with the village elders, and only just went to bed. Rygal has gone to check on Dandio."

Misty looked up at her, her eyes wide and worried. "Dusty—is Dandio going to be okay?"

Dusty turned to her and smiled faintly. "I think so, Misty. He has a good chance now that we're here. Don't worry."

The last few days had been so tense that now, safe at last, the familiar guilt rose in Mel's belly again, driving away his appetite. Images of Dandio holding back the serpentine, of its teeth tearing at him, blood streaking the ground as it attacked—the images floated through his mind, and sorrow choked his throat. Dandio had been ready to die to save him.

Misty left to explore the village. Mel remained in the hut, his thoughts gloomy and lonesome. He sat in the doorway with his chin in his hands, unable to shake the sudden heaviness that had clouded his mood.

Dusty approached so quietly he didn't hear her until she spoke. "It wasn't your fault, Mel."

Mel looked up at her quickly, then down at his hands. "You saw how it happened—if he had just left me out there—if he hadn't gone for the serpentine—none of this would of happened."

"And you would be dead now," Dusty told him quietly, sitting down beside him. "That's not Dandio's way, Mel. Your safety, your sister's safety—that was Dandio's priority. He'd have given his life for you before allowing it to kill you."

Mel kept his eyes down, not trusting himself to speak.

When Misty returned, Rygal was with her.

"He's doing better," Rygal said as they all started to ask. "Munben says they've stopped the effects of the venom. He's resting now, but I think he'll make it." The news lifted a weight of worry from Mel's chest.

"How soon can we leave, then?" Dusty asked.

"Not sure. Ask Glentree," Rygal said, taking a massive bite of bread to avoid answering more questions. This earned him a withering look from Dusty, and made Misty giggle.

The day passed slowly. Mel and Misty explored the village with Nella, who was eager to wander. The hama-dryads treated them with a quiet respect that threw Mel a little off guard. He realized that in their eyes, he was just as much a hero as Rygal and Dusty. Naturally, they didn't know that this was his first quest, or even his first time this far away from home.

They returned Nella to the stable and checked on the pony, then headed back toward the guest quarters, when Dusty appeared.

"Dandio's awake," she said.

They both followed her to the hospital hut, where Rygal and Glentree both waited. Munben-Lia met them outside and bowed slightly to them. "Welcome. Please come."

"Is…" Mel started, unsure of what to say.

"Come and see," the healer told him with a nod.

Dandio was sitting up on his cot, and smiled as the companions entered. He still looked very tired, but the color had come back to his face, and his eyes were lively and alert. "Good afternoon."

"How do you feel?" Mel asked anxiously.

"I'll live," Dandio said with that wry, half-smile that they knew so well.

Munben-Lia moved inside, studying Dandio carefully. "Well, well…you are still recovering. You must be careful not to overexert yourself." He checked the bandages, then nodded, seeming satisfied. "I have included medicine in your gear. It will help with the pain."

"Thank you," Dandio told him, looking up at the healer. "We are in your debt, sir. Once we return to Caer Sia, I will see to it that your tribe is rewarded."

Munben bowed, pleased by the praise. "We are glad to be of service to you, Lord Dandio. I might recommend that you rest a day longer before moving on again."

"Thank you, but no," Dandio said. "We must get back on the road. The Darkness is still on our trail, and Terrax may even now be closing in on Caer Sia. Drisilas must be returned."

"Very well," Munben said, inclining his head. "Then I wish you a safe journey, all of you." He looked at Dandio carefully. "Remember, your true hope in stopping the Darkness lies not in the sword, but in the heart. Remember the Stones."

Mel didn't understand what this cryptic message meant, and he could tell Rygal and Dusty didn't either. But Glentree and Dandio both seemed to know what he was talking about.

Glentree and Rygal loaded the gear onto the pack pony and harnessed Nella. Mel offered to help them, which gave him the opportunity to ask his question. "What are fireflowers, Glentree?"

The big man looked at him with a raised eyebrow. "How'd you know about them?"

"Um—Kalos mentioned it," Mel said quickly.

Glentree tightened the pony's girth. "Fireflowers are healing plants, Mel—some of the most valuable in the world, and the best way to treat internal injury. They're rare, too. But the tribe of Lia offered them willingly to heal Dandio."

Rygal looked at Glentree in surprise. "Fireflowers? Those *are* rare. How did Munben have any?"

"These northern woods are ideal for growing them," Glentree explained. "The Red Dawn uses them occasionally, for severe wounds. But like I said, they're hard to come by."

Dusty walked over with Misty. With them was Kalos-Lia. "We have restocked your supplies," the hama-dryad warrior said. He looked at Glentree. "My grandfather has warned me there may be trouble coming this way. I will prepare our warriors to fight."

"No," came Dandio's voice. The tall Liznee had approached soundlessly with Munben. "I appreciate everything you have done," he continued, smiling at the two hama-dryads. "But this danger is one you cannot fight on your own. Wait here until it is gone. You must trust me on this matter," he added firmly. Kalos looked a little disappointed, but at a nod from Munben, he agreed.

Munben studied the companions and smiled. "I am glad we were able to be of service, companions," he said. "May the High Light guard your steps."

Dandio clasped his hand. "I thank you again," he said. "Keep your people away from the main road. The Darkness may come through this way to reach Sia. Most likely, it will pass your village by, but I can't have your people pay the price should they challenge it."

"Then I will keep them here, safe," Munben promised, nodding.

By the time the sun had risen halfway in the sky, the six companions were on the road again, heading west.

18

Castle Sia

The final leg of the journey had begun, and the walk west was almost pleasant. Dandio strode purposefully in front of the group, showing no sign of having been injured. Seeing the Liznee recovered gave Mel a lightness in his chest that drove away his former gloom. The task was nearly complete. They would return the sword to Caer Sia, and everything would be all right again, because after that— after that they were going home.

It was a bright, sunny day, not a cloud in the sky. The wind rustled through the multicolored autumn leaves. Misty chattered happily to Dusty, who answered her with quiet patience like an older sister. Rygal and Glentree walked in the back, engaged in a heated debate about whether swords or maces were the best weapon.

"It *has* to be a sword, Glentree, they're easier to wield. Lighter and all around better."

"I could snap yer sword in two if I wanted to—you know this 'ere mace has won me more battles than a sword ever has."

"Have you ever *used* a sword in battle?"

"'Course not, silly things, felt like I was fighting with a toothpick…"

That left Mel to talk to Dandio. When they left the hama-dryad camp, he felt a nervous thrill and wondered if the Liznee begrudged him the injury. He was quickly reassured. Dandio's friendly manner dispelled his fear, and Mel relaxed.

"What do you do in Caer Sia?" he asked as they walked along.

"When I'm *not* having to go address threats elsewhere?" Dandio asked with a wry grin. "Oh, lots of things. Hunting when the weather allows. Sometimes my family and I sail to the Northern Isles of Gayrile and Kilee. In the winter months, it snows, and occasionally we have dogsled races." His eyes were distant as he stared down the road.

Mel realized that each quest was bittersweet for Dandio. Every time he started, he would be leaving behind his home, his family… everything he had was in Caer Sia. Thinking about that, Mel felt an ache of homesickness too.

Dandio coughed.

"Are you all right?" Mel asked anxiously.

The Liznee waved a hand absently. "I'm fine. Never better." But then he coughed again, and this time stumbled slightly.

Glentree was by them in a flash. "I think it'll be best if ya rest a bit, Dandio," he said. "The last thing you need is a relapse out here, 'specially with Sia still a ways off."

"No time," Dandio argued. "Once we're at Sia, there'll be rest for everyone."

"You might not make it to Sia, if you keep this up," Rygal put in. "And if you don't stop now, I'll knock you over the head with my sword and we'll tie you to the back of the pony again."

Dandio shook his head wearily. "You know, I *am* the High King's brother. Don't I get any respect?" But he agreed to stop for a break, and barely a minute after stopping, he laid down and slept.

Glentree roused them twenty minutes later, and they were soon back on the road. After about an hour passed, the path they had been following joined with a larger road heading north. This road was gravel, and there were fresh ruts left by wagons and carriages. Mel felt a slight thrill of excitement as he saw a signpost standing further down. They had reached the outskirts of Sia. In another moment, they crested the rise and looked down into the valley.

They stood on a hillock, looking down the gradually sloping hills into the city nestled in the valley. Beyond, sprawling on as far as Mel could see, lay Caer Sia. Simple wooden houses and buildings made up the city outskirts; closer to the center, the buildings were larger, elegantly built, some so tall they seemed to scrape the sky. Ahead and slightly to the right, Mel could see the sparkling coastline of the harbor. The wind blew the chilly sea air in his face, refreshing after the long journey.

Castle Sia was built just up from the harbor. The very architecture of the castle was foreign and extravagant to Mel's eyes. He was used to the simple, utilitarian designs of Daffodalion. Yet the castle before him seemed to be the very crown of the valley. Its elegant spires stood out above the skyline, taller than the tallest building in the city.

To the southeast on Mel's left, the foothills arched over the city below, densely forested. And towering over the picturesque scene were the Diamond Cap Mountains, purple-gray and powdered white with early snow. The river flowed gently down from the mountains, under the castle's drawbridge, and finally descending in a sparkling waterfall into the harbor.

It was the most beautiful city Mel had ever seen. "Wow," he said under his breath.

"Caer Sia," Dandio said in satisfaction. The tall Liznee stared out over the valley, eyes shining with contentment and love as he studied his home city.

They started down the gradually sloping road and passed through the farmlands before entering the city proper. The bustle of new sights and sounds took Mel's breath away. People walked along the edges of the roads, and carriages and horses hurried past. Dandio led them purposefully along the main road, towards the castle. Mel could catch snatches of excitement as people saw them: "Dandio Ki!" "It's Dandio Ki, he's back." "He's back!"

The news of their arrival carried through the city, a triumphant cry that never rose above a murmur. It meant that hope had returned. The sword had been returned.

In another half hour or so, they climbed up the slight slope to the castle. As they crossed the drawbridge, Mel looked back at the way they had come. He could view most all of the city from here. To the right, the sea stretched on as far as his eyes could see.

Castle Sia stood proudly as a perfect combination of elegance and practicality. The drawbridge was the main entrance into the central courtyard. Several smaller entrances with stone archways led down stone steps, leading to the stables and the servants' living quarters on the east side of the castle. To the west, the land sloped down slightly to the rocky beach a few miles from the main gate. In the other direction, the trees had been cleared to create a field about a mile wide. This, Mel guessed, prevented enemies from launching a surprise attack from the cover of the woods.

He looked up as the guards on the battlement above called a greeting. They had recognized Dandio as the companions entered the courtyard and saluted their commanding general. Dandio nodded and smiled in acknowledgment to them. Yet Mel noticed, at nearly the same moment, that all was not well in the city. The flag had been lowered to half-mast, a sign of trouble. He noticed the guards paced the walls worriedly, hands on their weapons.

War was no stranger to Sia.

The captain-of-guard, recognizable by his decorated uniform, moved to Dandio and stood at attention. "Welcome back, sir. I take it your mission was successful?"

"Indeed," Dandio said, smiling. "How fares everything here?"

The captain's grin faded slightly. "Better, now that you are back. The King can give you the particulars."

Dandio frowned at his worried tone, but the frown vanished as the door from the castle opened, and a teen girl entered the courtyard. With a joyful cry, she ran and embraced Dandio.

Dandio caught her in his arms, held her tightly, and smiled as she began talking rapidly.

"Father—we didn't hear—Jan said you would be back, but no one knew when, and we hadn't heard from you since you left Appledale."

"It's all right, Asescia. Is your mother here?"

"She got back from Badwater yesterday, she's giving her report to Jan. I'm so happy you're back, we didn't know if—"

"I'm here," Dandio told her, hugging her tightly again. He released her and turned to the others. "For those of you who haven't met—this is my daughter, Asescia."

"You can call me Allie," the young Liznee said with a friendly grin. She had the same twinkling green eyes as her father, set in a youthful face eager to smile.

"Hi," Mel said. Misty was too in awe of meeting a real princess to say anything, and just stared.

Allie turned back to Dandio. "Dad—you won't believe what happened here while you were gone. We figured out who hired Terrax and Adderstrike. It was Drona—our Pellion Drona!"

Mel didn't recognize this name, but both Glentree and Dandio looked thunderstruck. "Pellion?" Dandio repeated at last, stunned.

"Yes! All this time, Dad, he's been working against us. He wanted the throne, and he's…" she hesitated, then finished. "He's trying to bring the Darkness here. But we haven't seen or heard anything from him since he escaped on Adderstrike."

Dandio shook his head slowly in disbelief. Glentree looked at Allie, out of words. "How'd you figure all that out?" the big man stammered finally.

"Oh! Well, he tried to kill me—Jan kept me safe, though. I'm *fine*, Dad," she added wearily as Dandio snapped out of his shock at her words.

"You're all right?" Dandio demanded, looking her up and down for injury.

"Yes, I'm fine," Allie repeated patiently.

Dandio seemed satisfied, but hugged her tightly again. "Filthy traitor," he hissed, shaking his head. "He'll pay for that. I'll kill him myself for it."

"Jan said you'd say that," Allie said.

"Jan said he would keep you safe," Dandio said, frowning. "Doesn't sound like you were safe…"

"Jan said you'd say that too," Allie said with another grin. "Don't be mad at him. I'm all right, I promise."

They walked inside the palace. Mel looked at the young princess, curious to know who they were talking about. "Who's Pellion?" he asked finally. The name was vaguely familiar.

"He was Jan's steward and advisor," Allie explained. "He was helping us investigate the whole issue with Terrax—but turns out he's been the one pulling the strings all this time."

Rygal looked at her with a slight frown. "And you think he's working for the Darkness too?"

"He's not working for it, not as far as we can tell. He wants to lure the Darkness here, have it do the dirty work for him. And then he'll rule whatever is left," Allie said grimly.

Dusty raised her eyebrows. "That won't work for him. The Darkness won't differentiate between him and the people he wants it to kill. It will kill everyone, Drona included."

"That's what Jan told me," Allie said. She looked at the fierce Wildkid, impressed. "You're Dusty? Rygal told me about you."

Dusty threw a look at Rygal, but she looked pleased.

They walked through the doors into the palace. Ajaha, Dandio's wife, stood in the hall, giving instructions to a group of well-dressed people. She looked tired, and sounded rather exasperated. But when she turned and saw Dandio, the weariness seemed to fall away—she walked away from the other couriers in the middle of their complaint and rushed to her husband. Dandio stepped toward her and embraced her tightly, both of them forgetting everything else, and kissed her for a long moment.

Mel looked away. Misty sighed dreamily. The others watched the scene with a happy satisfaction.

And then, from outside, the horn of the watchmen began to sound in alarm. The voices of the guards on the battlement came distantly to Mel's ears, raised in urgent concern.

Dandio looked up sharply. "That's the south wall," he said slowly.

"Terrax?" Glentree growled.

"Or worse," Dandio murmured. He looked at Ajaha, clearly pained to leave her.

"Go, and be safe," Ajaha told him simply. "I'll find Jan."

"Stay off the walls," Dandio told her, kissing her brow. Then he turned, back to business. "Glentree, find Captain Leopold and Captain Elris. Tell them to get their men set up and ready on the walls. Prepare the cannons."

Glentree nodded and jogged off down the hall. Mel hesitated, not sure how to help. The city was on the brink of war. That meant he would probably only get in the way, he and Misty both. But he wanted to help somehow. It felt wrong to have worked so hard to get here only to wait and hide while the Liznees battled for their lives.

But he knew where his responsibility lay first. "Misty, you should go with Lady Ajaha," he said, gripping his sister's hand.

Misty looked up at him with wide eyes. "What are you going to do?"

"I'll be there in a little bit, too," Mel promised, not sure what he *was* going to do. He reached up and tugged on the tall Liznee woman's sleeve hesitantly. "Could you take my sister somewhere safe? While the battle's happening?"

Kindness sparkled in Ajaha's eyes, and she nodded. "Of course, child. But where are you going?"

"I—the sword," Mel stammered. Drisilas needed to be returned. He had received the sword back in Appledale. He had joined the quest with the purpose of returning it. It was time to see that venture through to the end. But he didn't think he could put that into words, and only squeezed Misty's hand in farewell before running after Dandio.

· · · · · ·

Jan stood on the south wall, giving instructions to the guards who waited there. The alarm had been sounded prematurely, he could tell. Apparently a young scout had brought back news of a large host marching towards Caer Sia from the south. But they had yet to see any signs of the army, or to judge if the group was hostile or not.

Despite this, Jan had issued an order to evacuate the south side of the city. The last thing he wanted was for the civilians to be drawn into the fighting. Terrax still held a bit of honor—his heritage as a descendant of Liridox bound him to the rules of fair combat. But

Adderstrike was a murderer, and would kill simply for the sport of it.

He turned as Dandio appeared. "Good to see you back," he said with a smile.

"Had to find your sword," Dandio said with the same grin. The two brothers embraced, forgetting formalities for a moment. Then Dandio straightened, back to business. "What's the situation up here?"

"Nothing yet," Jan said. "Pellion is smart. He won't order Terrax to attack until the opportune moment. And I assume he will try to use Adderstrike as a distraction, like last time."

"Probably," Dandio murmured. "But we might have a worse problem on our hands than them."

Jan looked at him carefully. "Were the rumors… confirmed?" he asked at length.

Dandio paused, then nodded slowly. "It's back, Jan. It… it killed Llyrion." There was a silence. Jan looked at him in shock. "That Star-Stone in Drisilas is the only chance we have," Dandio said finally. "I don't know how we'll stop it… but you know as well as I do that we can't stop it with mortal weapons."

"Soldiers to the south, sir!" one of the guards shouted, interrupting the conversation.

"How many?" Dandio asked, moving to the wall where the man stood.

"Maybe a hundred, maybe more," the guard said, pointing.

"Soldiers to the east as well, sir," another soldier reported. His voice was strained and tense.

Dandio's eyes scanned the woods below. Through the trees, he could catch glimpses of movement. There was no glinting armor, no chainmail. These would be Terrax's ruffians, clad in plain leather armor and tattered clothes. Come to fight for the spoils that Terrax's victory would bring.

It was impossible to guess how many from this distance, and with the thick cover of trees that protected them. They had nearly reached the wide open strip that stood as a barrier between the forest and the castle, which protected them from a sneak attack. Once the approaching enemy came into the light, he could better gauge what would be done in counter attack.

Then, just as the thought crossed his mind, the sound of heavy wings reached his ears, and a massive shadow fell over them. A kragon descended on the far end of the wall, some twenty paces from the waiting guards, snarling softly. Adderstrike had come.

And sliding easily off his back, a smirk on his face, was Pellion Drona.

. . . . . .

Mel had almost reached the wall when he heard the low thump of something heavy landing above, followed by a menacing growl. For a moment he hesitated, unsure of what to do. Then curiosity overcame him, and he walked the rest of the way up to the wall.

A huge creature crouched on the far end of the wall, facing the ready guards, who had pointed their weapons at it in unison. Dandio stood in front of them, one hand raised, warning the soldiers not to attack yet. The scaled creature facing them growled again, softly. There was an intelligent yet maddened glint in the yellow eyes. Mel knew immediately that this was Adderstrike, the rebel kragon.

A man had dismounted the kragon, and now faced Dandio, his arms folded over his chest as he studied them. "Dandio," he said finally, his voice dripping with sarcasm. "How very… nice to see you again."

"You dare threaten my daughter?" Dandio snarled.

"Why did you come back, Drona?" Jan asked at the same time, his voice carrying over the walls.

Drona rolled his eyes. "Oh, really, you don't know why I'm back? Not that you were ever as wise as people say you are."

"Coming from a man who stole a sword he knew only one could wield, your insult is ironic," Jan said calmly, a faint smile touching his features. "But you haven't answered my question. Why are you here?"

Drona's face reddened in anger. "I have come to offer you one chance. One chance only to surrender and turn the city over to me, before the Darkness comes and destroys it all."

"Is that so," Jan said quietly, still calm. Drona's words had had an effect on the guards; they looked at their king in surprise and fear at the mention of the Darkness.

Mel stepped up on the wall slowly and stood a little ways behind Dandio, watching and listening.

"I know you value the lives of these peasants," Drona spat. "Thus, your only chance is to surrender. Now, before I allow Adderstrike to feast on their pathetic flesh." The kragon growled softly behind him, the hideous face contorting in a wickedly toothy smile. Mel felt his stomach lurch with fear and revulsion.

"You will pay," Drona continued, his voice rising. "You will all pay for your treachery. I was cheated! I deserved a crown—a crown that will go to that brat of a girl when you are dead, Ĵan. It can't be a surprise that I wish her death above even yours." He smiled.

"And that is why you fail," Ĵan told him. "Greed is dangerous, Drona. So are false promises. What sort of lies have you told yourself recently…about the Darkness?"

Drona frowned slightly, confused by the change in topic. "The Darkness? Ah yes, the Darkness…well, Ĵan, a little awkward explanation for your soldiers is in order. The Darkness is back. And unfortunately, bringing the sword back has led it straight here."

The soldiers were worried now, shifting uncertainly and glancing questions in Dandio's direction. Mel could sense their fear. Many of them were experienced soldiers. They knew exactly what the Darkness would do once it came, just like Dandio did.

"I do not see the Darkness here yet, Drona," Ĵan said simply. "And playing the role of a puppeteer will prove a very dangerous mistake for you, I promise you that. You have pulled too many strings—in another moment, you will be entangled."

Drona smirked. "You think the Darkness will turn on me? I *highly* doubt that, Ĵan. I've given it no reason to do that. In fact, it will be grateful to me, after all the times I've practically gifted Dandio and his companions to it." He scowled. "It could have killed them many a time, foolish creature. It did kill the Elf, I was told."

"You beast," Dandio hissed, stepping forward. The mention of Llyrion had broken his restraint.

Jan held him back, his eyes still on Drona. "You think the Darkness works with allies? That it will keep you alive only because you haven't hindered it in its conquest? Drona, the Darkness is a force of destruction, not a being to be reasoned with. It cannot coexist with anything that threatens its power. Once it takes Sia, it will kill you too, and all who follow you. You are a fool to think anything differently."

For the first time a trace of doubt crossed Drona's face. "Pretty words, Jan," he muttered. "But I have not come here to hear warnings. You have one chance, and one chance only—lay down your weapons and surrender. The Darkness is coming, and it will soon be night."

Adderstrike growled again, this time an eager sound. There was the sound of footsteps on the stairs, and Mel turned to see Rygal and Glentree appear.

"What's happening here?" Rygal asked softly.

"Drona's here—he's trying to make us surrender. He thinks the Darkness is on his side," Mel whispered. That pretty much summed it up.

Drona stood tall, waiting for a reply. Jan said nothing, his expression calm. Drona finally flushed angrily and turned away. "Do not say that I did not warn you, Jan. My army is coming."

He climbed back on Adderstrike's back and they flew away, joining the east group of warriors. A few guards fired half-hearted arrows after them, but the kragon dodged them nimbly.

Dandio turned back to the soldiers. "He's coming back soon, and Terrax will be with him. We must set up a barrier around the city. Draw them out to fight on the field to the northwest—we don't want battle in the streets."

"The Darkness," one of the guards said slowly, sounding worried. "He said the Darkness is back."

"Is that true?" another man asked.

Dandio took a deep breath. "It's true. We must be prepared. With all luck we can defeat Drona before the Darkness arrives, and lead it away again."

There was a shout from one of the guards, who was pointing out to the east. "Sire, look—it's Terrax, he's coming!"

Mel peered through the shuffling bodies to see a host of warriors approaching from the east. Adderstrike's huge form stalked across the ground before them, leading Terrax's army to the castle.

"Where did he get all those warriors?" he asked Rygal as he moved to get a better look.

"Caer Sia has no shortage of enemies," Rygal said grimly. "Most likely Terrax rounded them up as he journeyed here."

More alarms—trumpets blared from the towers, warning the civilians. Dandio shouted orders to the soldiers, and they waited, tense in the sudden silence as the warriors drew closer.

Then Jan's hand rested on Rygal's shoulder. "The sword," the king said, looking them urgently. "Where is Drisilas?"

Rygal and Mel exchanged a startled glance. In the midst of all that had happened, they had left Drisilas strapped to Nella's back, and allowed Nella to be led away to the stables—

The most unprotected part of the castle.

"We'll get it!" Rygal said, and jogged down the stairs into the castle. Mel hurried after him.

They wove their way through the castle and past crowds of worried courtiers and soldiers. Finally they pushed through the doors and into the courtyard. Rygal led the way to the east side of the courtyard and out a side door. They jogged down a short flight of stone steps. Muted conversation came from the guards on the battlement directly above them, and Mel saw them pointing. He followed their gaze; through the trees, he caught glimpses of Drona's army, moving steadily toward the castle.

The stable was built on the side of the castle walls, medium sized and shaped like an octagon, and housed many, many horses. The smell of horse filled Mel's nose as they ran through the halls before Rygal skidded to a halt. Nella was curled up on a bed of straw, her gear unloaded neatly beside her. Drisilas, held in a burlap sack, leaned against the wall.

"Stupid stable hands," Rygal muttered, as Mel lifted the sword.

"Got it!"

"Let's go—hurry."

Mel could hear shouting drawing closer, the marching of many feet. They ran back through the stables, towards the door.

The battle was starting, he realized. They had to return Drisilas to Jan if there was any hope of defeating the Darkness—

"Watch out!" Rygal's shout made Mel freeze as they left the door—Rygal shoved him back in the same instant that Adderstrike's tail whipped into him, flinging him back. There was a sickening crack as Rygal hit the solid rock wall.

"Rygal!" Mel shouted in alarm, shrinking back into the shadow of the building as the huge kragon moved toward his friend.

The kragon snarled, towering over them, saliva dripping from the tip of his curved beak. Mel rushed forward and swung Drisilas in its scabbard at the kragon's face. Adderstrike growled again and took a step closer. Mel froze, clutching the sword, heart pounding in terror as he waited for the huge beast to strike him down.

In that moment, several things happened at once.

Someone shouted—Mel heard Drona's voice, the words too distant to make out clearly, jumbled in confusion and anger. Then he heard someone scream.

Mel looked toward Terrax's approaching warriors.

In a moment that was burned into his mind forever, one that would haunt his nightmares for years to come, Terrax's soldiers stopped, as though they had run into an invisible wall. Then they began to fall. Terrax, in the lead, turned and stared in shock as his warriors crumbled, some crying out, others ominously silent. Then their screams of fear and agony filled the air—both the horrified watchers from the walls, and the dying soldiers on the ground. Terrax staggered back, watching in horror as his soldiers crumpled. Black fog seeped through the cracks in their leather armor, the last glimmer of their life draining away.

In near unison, hundreds of Terrax's men lay dead in their armor, their charred skulls grinning up at their leader.

"What sorcery is this, Liznee?" Drona screamed up at the towers. On the other side of the field, Terrax stepped away from the charred bodies. Mel could see the shock on his face as he realized, for the first time, that he had drastically miscalculated the situation. But few were looking at Terrax anymore. Something else had emerged from the woods where the warriors had come from.

Black fog was spreading through the woods, moving towards the castle. Mel watched in horror, waiting in silence as the shadows drew close, knowing, somehow, what was happening.

There were no tricks, no illusions, no uncertainty this time. The Darkness had come.

19

The Wraith of Night

Adderstrike snarled and sprang away from the stables to join Drona, leaving Rygal on the ground gasping for breath. Mel gripped Rygal's arm, trying to raise him. But he was unable to tear his eyes away from the horror that had appeared at the far end of the field.

He wasn't sure what he had expected the Darkness to look like. Maybe a tall figure robed in black, or a wraith-like form with a giant sword. Those few vague images had crossed his mind during times when he had speculated what they might face.

The Darkness didn't look like either of his ideas. What was sweeping across the field toward the city seemed to be a cloud of rapidly growing mist. Even that didn't define it, though, because mist was slightly transparent… and the approaching menace was black, pure black, a void of nothingness, as if a blotch of ink had fallen and blotted the scene before them. At the fog's center stood a vague shape of a stooped figure, cloaked and hooded. Yet that shape continuously shifted and changed with every moment it drew closer, altering its appearance to best combat anyone fool enough to challenge it. The toxic black fog that had recently claimed the lives of Terrax's warriors swirled around its frame as it came, a whirling, silent, twisting maelstrom of pure destruction.

No wonder Dandio feared it so.

Drona was shouting for a retreat—the group of warriors behind him did so without hesitation, returning to the shelter of the trees. Terrax ran towards them too, narrowly avoiding the black wraith as it swept across the field. Drona's face was pale with fear, and Mel knew that he finally understood that he held no control over what was happening.

The Darkness had paused in the center of the field, its entire frame shivering with the energy it had absorbed from the unfortunate outlaws. Its invisible eyes swept over the castle, surveying the scene. Panic filled Mel—they were unprotected here, exposed.

"Rygal," he gasped, clutching the young warrior's shoulder frantically. "Rygal, please get up—we have to run—"

Rygal lay on his back, wincing at every ragged, painful breath. He was twisted at an odd angle—Mel was pretty sure something had been broken by Adderstrike's blow. But they couldn't stay here—the Darkness was coming.

He glanced over his shoulder—the wraith's attention was fixed on the castle, where Caer Sia's warriors watched in horror. It hadn't seen Drisilas—yet—but once it did, they would all be dead.

"Rygal…come on…" Mel moaned through gritted teeth, his heart pounding.

Rygal tried to sit up, but gave a groan of pain and fell back. Mel put an arm around him and half-hauled him to a sitting position. The motion made the young warrior give a choked cry. Mel looked over quickly, but the Darkness hadn't heard them.

"Come on…" he whispered, putting an arm under Rygal's so that he was supporting him. Rygal was taller than Mel was, and quite a bit heavier too—Mel strained under the weight as they got to their feet. Finally they stood, both of them out of breath, and began edging toward the stairs that led back into the castle courtyard.

"My lord!" Drona's voice, shrill from both fear and excitement, rang out, and Mel looked over abruptly. Drona pointed directly at them. "The sword! He is the one who brought the sword!"

The Darkness swung around to face them—a consuming chill of fear unlike any Mel had ever felt ran down his spine as it began to approach.

"No, no, no," Rygal groaned, stumbling to his knees again.

The mist crept towards them purposefully. From his place in the woods, Drona smiled in satisfaction. Mel dragged Rygal another few steps and then fell, exhausted, panic surging through his body as he faced the approaching death.

Then a blast of crackling red shot from behind him, over their heads and into the center of the Darkness. The wraith reeled back under the powerful force, an otherworldly hiss issuing from its invisible mouth.

Jan and Dandio sprang down the courtyard steps, red lightning crackling and shining from their hands as they attacked side by side, firing again and again at the towering wraith. And, amazingly, the Darkness fell back, the sudden attack forcing it to give ground. But only for a moment—Mel saw four black, claw-like hands emerge from the depths of the void. White ice shot from the palms, sending the two Liznees leaping out of the way.

Yet the brief distraction had been enough—Mel dragged Rygal forward to the steps. Glentree met him almost immediately, supporting the young warrior inside the courtyard to safety. As he did, Ĵan fired a second shot that set the shrubbery at the base of the steps up in flames. The Darkness fell back slowly at the sight of the fire, and the two brothers ran back up into the courtyard before the fire sealed them out.

"Cannons!" Dandio shouted hoarsely—at the command, the air exploded in a series of deafening blasts. Mel covered his ears and watched as the turf in front of the Darkness was ripped apart by the cannon fire. The black wraith reeled back, vanishing into the cloud of smoke and scattered grass and soil.

Leaning against the wall, Dandio grinned slightly at the rumble of cannon fire. "We didn't have *those* the last time it was here," he chuckled weakly to himself.

"No, we didn't," Ĵan agreed with a faint smile. "How are you doing?"

"Fine, just fine," Dandio said with a slow shrug. The motion made him wince, and he rubbed his shoulder gingerly. "A bit sore," he admitted as Ĵan raised an eyebrow. "Serpentine venom—don't recommend. But I can fight."

"Good. I still need you," Ĵan told him with a half-smile. "Gather your strength for now." He turned back to the field. On the far edge of the clearing, Drona, Terrax, and the remaining warriors had ventured out slowly, watching as the smoke cleared. The flames at the edge of the steps still burned, barring the way up into the castle. At least from that direction—Mel doubted the Darkness would be stopped by the small flames.

They watched the battlefield through the flames at the doorway. Allie and Dusty had joined them, all watching in silence.

The Darkness was visible again now. It stood a few paces back from the smoldering crater made by the cannons, silently watching. Unharmed by the cannon fire, and preparing to attack.

Allie looked up at her father. "What should we do?"

"You need to stay here," Dandio told her briskly. "Out of the battle and in the safety of the castle. This is not the time for you to fight."

Allie raised an eyebrow. "Our entire world is at stake. Seems like a pretty decent time to—"

"Asescia—please. Stay out of the battle," Dandio ordered, squeezing her shoulders. The young princess met his gaze but finally looked away, her brow wrinkled in disappointment.

Dandio straightened, loosening his sword in its scabbard, and looked at Jan. "Ready?"

"Whenever you are," his brother replied, and drew Drisilas out of the scabbard in a flaming arc. Yellow fire played down the blade, licking along the steel, pure light and heat and energy radiating from Drisilas' core. The two Liznees sprang back down the steps, red light in their palms, Dandio's sword reflecting Drisilas' fire.

Despite himself, Mel grinned in awe.

Drona watched, his face twisted with hate as the two Liznees moved forward side-by-side—Mel saw him turn to Terrax, yelling angrily, then turn back to face the battle. "Charge!"

There was a moment of hesitation from his throng of warriors before they surged forward in siege of Castle Sia.

"We have to help," Mel murmured anxiously.

Glentree moved back towards the stairs that led up to the battlement above, bellowing orders to the gunners. Cannon fire rained down upon the charging warriors. The first line of outlaws were felled instantly by the first charge; in the space it took to reload the cannons, Terrax led the others forward under the cannons' trajectory.

"Hold down the east gates!" the captain shouted. A garrison of soldiers brushed past the watching companions by the doorway, rushing to meet the onslaught of attackers in the field beyond. There were so many attackers—far more than Mel had thought originally. And they were fighting ferociously. Either they hated the Liznees enough to risk their lives, or they were being paid enough by Drona to fight. Mel guessed both.

"What do we do?" he asked anxiously. Glentree had gone up on the walls, Rygal was injured, and Jan and Dandio were engaged in battling the black wraith beyond. That left him, Dusty, and Allie.

Dusty bent her bow back behind her leg to string it, her jaw set. "You any good with that?" she asked, jerking her head at the sword Allie had at her side.

"I'm—yes, but I've never actually fought anyone in combat," the Liznee princess stammered.

"Good enough. Let's go." Dusty turned, striding down the steps to the raging battle outside, an arrow fitted to her bowstring and her quiver slung ready at her side. Behind her came Allie, gripping her short bladed sword, her face pale with fear but filled with determination. Mel watched as they sprang down to clash with another onslaught of Terrax's warriors who had reached the castle walls. Two fell to Dusty's arrows, and Allie injured a third warrior before he could reach the castle.

"I figured they'd get along well," Rygal said hoarsely. He stood unsteadily, leaning against the stone wall beside the doorway for support, watching the unfolding conflict outside. He held his sword loosely.

Mel stood beside him and watched as the two opposing groups clashed on the battlefield. The air filled with the cacophony of clanging weapons, the cries and curses from the injured, and the muffled grunts and panting of people fighting for their lives. Terrax led his remaining warriors, but Mel could tell a little of the fire had gone out of him. Seeing the Darkness, a creature he had assumed was on his side, decimate half of his forces had definitely shaken him.

"I'm going out there," Rygal said, taking a tentative step forward. He winced and fell awkwardly back against the wall, clutching his side with his free hand.

Mel quickly went to help him. "No—Rygal, you can't fight like this. Stay here—the Red Dawn can handle Terrax."

The Red Dawn Army of Caer Sia were the best fighting force in the west, Mel knew. Despite the numbers that Terrax's outlaws had, they didn't have the skill and experience of the Liznee soldiers.

"I know they can handle Terrax," Rygal panted, taking another painful breath as he sat down. "But the Darkness—we have to stop it. And the Liznees… they'll need all the help they can get."

"Watch out!" Glentree's deep voice shouted a warning from above just in time—Mel flattened himself against the wall as a hail of icy darts flew from the Darkness' claw-like hands and embedded themselves in the rock walls beside him. Two soldiers cried out in pain from above; Mel saw them drop to their knees on the battlement. Two others lay still and silent, their chests glistening with pale ice.

"Fall back!" came Dandio's voice from across the field. "To the walls—slowly—"

Mel risked a glimpse outside again. Bodies lay scattered across the field, bodies of the soldiers and Terrax's outlaws. He saw Drona in the safety of the trees on the far end of the field, watching with satisfaction. The Darkness remained where it was, hovering slightly in the center of the battlefield. It had grown larger, darker, the swirling mist around it scorching the grass. Maybe it was just the angle… or maybe it was growing stronger.

The Red Dawn soldiers pushed past him into the courtyard. "Where's Dusty?" Mel asked of no one in particular, his question drowned out by many other voices. More and more soldiers entered the courtyard, some supporting the wounded bodies of their comrades. Doctors had come out of the castle and were tending to the wounded. More voices filled the air, drowning out Mel's calls for Dusty as his panic grew.

Then, finally, he saw them. Allie, supporting Dusty inside the courtyard. The Wildkid was bleeding heavily from a long gash that ran down the length of her leg. Blood matted her dark fur, and she was gasping for breath. A medic met them at the entrance, and quickly took her away for treatment.

"Is she all right?" Rygal demanded immediately as Allie sat down heavily beside them.

"Yes, I think so. It wasn't the outlaws. We were fighting them just fine. Then the Darkness shot all that—ice—at us. It hit everyone. It doesn't care if Drona's warriors were on its side."

"Drona was never on its side," Rygal said, shaking his head. "He just thought he was."

"Yes, well, Terrax knows that now. I doubt it will go well for Drona." Allie frowned. "Are you all right?"

"Just fine," Rygal said with a crooked grin. "How do you like battle?"

The princess let out a long breath. "It's not what I pictured," she said finally.

Mel agreed inwardly. His mind had created different ideas of what a full-out battle would look like. Reality was much less glorious, much more violent. "Where's Jan and Dandio?" he asked, realizing he hadn't seen them come in.

Allie stood swiftly and moved to the doorway, looking out across the field. Mel saw her expression tighten with fear. "I see them— they're on the far edge of the clearing. I think they're retreating the other way, into the woods."

Rygal looked up worriedly. "There's nowhere for them to go over there. This is the safest place to be—why didn't they come back here?"

"I… I think they're trying to draw the Darkness away from the city." Allie's voice trembled with worry. Mel peeked outside— he could see the distant forms of the two Liznees fading into the shadowed woods. The Darkness had fixed its attention on them.

"Do you think they'll destroy it?" he asked hopefully. If the Darkness drew its power from the destruction of the city, then maybe it could be destroyed once it was far enough away.

"They can't destroy it, not completely," Rygal said, shaking his head. "Drisilas is the only thing that might be able to do that, but we don't even know how to use it."

"Jan will," Mel said, hoping he was right. But he had seen Jan fighting with Drisilas during the whole battle—and while the sword seemed to infuriate the black wraith, it didn't do any noticeable sort of damage.

Unless it wasn't about Drisilas… unless it was about something else…

"Your true hope in stopping the Darkness lies not in the sword, but in the heart. Remember the Stones."

Munben-Lia's words flooded Mel's mind, and now, suddenly, they began to make sense. The heart. Not an actual physical heart, it meant the heart of the sword's power, the Star-Stone Isilas, gifted to the Liznees so long ago—

The Stone must be the key to stop the Darkness.

But how? Could it be removed from the sword's hilt somehow? Mel had no idea what a stone could do to stop such a threat as this, but he knew they had to try.

"Rygal, remember what Munben said—about the Stone—" he stammered, trying to put his ideas into words. The solution was right on the tip of his tongue; he was infuriatingly close to understanding, he felt it. "He said if we're going to stop the Darkness, the way to do it is the heart of Drisilas. It's about the Star-Stone."

Rygal shifted his weight against the wall and winced again, putting a hand against his side. "The Stone… but why? And how is that supposed to help anything?"

"Remember what Dandio told us about the Stars and Nihm-Lia?" Mel pressed on. "The Star-Stone has more power than we think. The Darkness can't touch Drisilas because of the Stone, and it's protected by its own powers. But if Jan can get closer—into that—" he pointed at the swirling void that surrounded the wraith, "then the Stone's power will defeat it."

"Wait," Allie said, catching onto the idea. "If Drisilas' stone came from the Stars, that's why the Darkness fears it. It's not about the sword—the true power was *always* in the Stone. That's how we'll stop it."

Mel looked back across the field. He saw Jan and Dandio, red lightning sparking from their fingertips occasionally as they continued to battle the black wraith. But they were tiring—he could tell. And while Drisilas kept the Darkness at bay, Jan couldn't get close enough for the Stone's power to affect it.

Not if he was combating the Darkness with the blade… not like that. Not without someone else to draw its attention away, if only for a moment.

The realization dawned on him, and he swallowed hard, mouth dry. This was it. He knew exactly what would attract the Darkness' attention—the prey it had been seeking ever since the sword arrived in Appledale. It wanted *him*. An eleven-year-old, inexperienced boy, trembling at the very idea. But he knew, with startling certainty, that this was the truth. Nor did he feel afraid. This was how they would defeat the Darkness. After all this time, after all that had been lost, he knew this was their chance.

"I know what to do," he said, taking a deep breath.

Rygal's face paled as he realized what Mel planned to do. "No, Mel—it's too dangerous—"

Mel stood and gripped the hilt of his dagger. "I'm going to draw its attention. Maybe if I give Jan enough time, he can get close enough to kill it."

"Mel—" Allie began desperately.

Mel turned and sprang down the steps to the charred field beyond. The moment his shoes hit the grass, he was running, toward the sparse trees that were all that remained of the woods. His eyes fixed on the swirling cloud of black mist that made up the wraith ahead.

Then a cold hand gripped the back of his collar and flung him back. "You!" hissed a familiar voice. Drona towered over him, his eyes wild with maddened rage. "*You're* the little brat who ruined my plans. The sword would have been lost for good had not you interfered."

Mel jumped to his feet and raised his dagger. The blade felt awkward in his hands, but he tried to hide his uncertainty. "Let me pass, Drona," he said, as firmly as he could manage.

Drona gave a short laugh. "Or what, you'll kill me? I can see it in your eyes. You don't have it in you."

Something moved behind Drona, approaching. Mel lowered his blade. "You're right. I don't."

Drona laughed again and took a step closer. Then a blade whipped around him, flattening against his throat as he was hauled backward into a grip like steel. Mel jumped back, shocked.

Terrax pressed the blade of his knife against Drona's neck. "My pay, traitor," he hissed in the former steward's ear. "You lied to me about the sword. My men have paid the price."

"You should have left while you had the chance," Drona snarled.

"Is that a no?" the Elven outlaw asked, voice still low.

Drona laughed softly and shook his head. "There is no kingdom for you to inherit," he said. "The Darkness will leave you nothing but ashes."

Terrax slashed his throat, and Drona's body fell to the ground in a heap. Mel jumped back fearfully as the outlaw's dark eyes fixed on him. There was a tense silence, then Terrax wiped his dagger clean on his cloak and snapped the blade back into its sheath. "Go," he ordered sharply. "You foiled his plans once. Might be able to do it again, I dare say."

And so saying, he turned, leading the remnants of his warriors into the eastern woods.

Mel watched as they left, startled. Terrax had retreated. Drona was dead. That left only the Darkness. What the Elven outlaw had said echoed in his mind and renewed his determination. It was time to finish the quest.

Mel turned away and continued forward. His presence must have been sensed. In a whirling cloud of pure shadow, the Darkness turned until its hidden eyes trained on him.

Prey.

20

The Stone of Drisilas

Mel stopped in his tracks on the field beyond the castle, watching as the Darkness approached. The wraith moved slowly, almost uncertainly, as though confused as to why a mere boy had come to challenge it. The grass withered under its unseen feet, and the swirling fog around it continued to swell, growing larger and larger until the Darkness towered over them.

A flash of red lightning struck it from behind, and Ĵan stepped out of the trees, one hand lowered at the Darkness, the other gripping Drisilas. Flames ran up and down the length of the blade. "Keep back," he warned as the Darkness turned away from Mel to face him again. A hail of icy darts shot from the Darkness' many hands, and Ĵan sprang out of the way just in time.

"No—let it come!" Mel yelled back to him.

Dandio moved to Mel's side, staring in shock and awe at the towering black wraith. Drawing strength from the deaths it had brought about, the Darkness had grown like a thundercloud made of shadow and ice. It towered over them, nearly the size of the palace.

"Light above," Dandio murmured under his breath.

Mel turned to him, taking a breath to steady his nerves. "Dandio, remember what Munben told us. Our best chance at stopping that thing is the Star-Stone. If it's after me—if I can distract it, there's a good chance Jan can get close enough to destroy it."

Dandio looked uncertain, but didn't protest. "All right… I'll help you. What do you—"

Before he could finish the question, a huge shape soared down from the sky, letting out a cry of rage. They had forgotten about Adderstrike. Thinking back later, Mel guessed he had remained hidden on the edges of the battle, waiting for the opportune time to strike. Now, angered by Drona's failed plan, he dove straight at Jan. The king, already off balance from the Darkness' last attack, dropped flat just in time. Adderstrike's talons clawed for the sword, missed, and instead slashed a cut in Jan's arm.

The Darkness turned to face the kragon, firing a bolt of white ice after Adderstrike's tail. The kragon dropped out of the way, then with another shriek of fury, he turned to dive again, this time at Dandio and Mel.

"Get back!" Dandio warned, and Mel took shelter behind him. Red lightning flashed in Dandio's hands, and he fired a blast straight at the kragon's face. Adderstrike lurched in the sky with a cry of pain, landing awkwardly on the ground as he tried to paw at his injured face. But he recovered quickly, and lifted into the sky again. Mel could see the rage and madness in his bloodshot yellow eyes. Outmatched or no, Adderstrike was clearly prepared to fight till the end.

But the end came quicker than anyone expected. As Adderstrike lifted into the sky, preparing for another dive, Mel saw a second winged shape sweeping down through the clouds. A second kragon, larger even than Adderstrike, had arrived, the dying sunlight glinting on a band of gold he wore on his huge head. Mel stared in awe as the second kragon crashed into Adderstrike, talons digging into the other's scaled skin. The two tackled each other midair, snarling and slashing.

"Hurry!" Dandio urged. Mel tore his eyes away from the bloody battle unraveling above them. While he had never seen the second kragon before, he knew without a doubt that it was the kragon lord—Fireclaw. The sheer size and strength of the kragon lord was fearsome to behold as he tore relentlessly at Adderstrike, opening great wounds in his body. Still Adderstrike fought, clawing and shrieking in rage. Yet he was overcome—Fireclaw's soldiers had come now, some swooping low to carry the remaining wounded to safety, others joining their lord in battle against the one who had betrayed them.

The Darkness had been distracted by the battling kragons for a moment, but now turned back to Ĵan. The king stood just within of the trees, gripping Drisilas. Blood streamed down his arm from the gash left by Adderstrike's claws.

Mel tightened his grip on his dagger. His hands were clammy with fear, which made it harder to hold on. But he stepped forward, one foot in front of the other, closer to the swirling cloud that surrounded the wraith. He kept his eyes on the Darkness, willing himself to continue. And now the Darkness noticed him—the toxic mist swirled as the towering wraith swept forward.

Mel gripped his dagger with both hands, holding it a little in front of his face, watching as the Darkness approached. Through the fog, he saw Ĵan straighten, shock on his face as he saw what Mel was doing. He thought he heard Dandio call his name, though the voice was lost in the blur as the Darkness reached him.

Mel didn't hesitate. This was the way he would finish it all; this was the way he would repay those who had sacrificed to save him. Reckoning had come.

Cold gray hands like a corpse's appeared from the Darkness' shapeless form. The fog enveloped him as the wraith drew closer, burning cold, and seared his skin. Mel gathered another ragged breath into his lungs. His heart throbbed in his chest. It was becoming harder to see as he looked up.

Through the howling winds that filled the mist, he saw the Darkness. Bent slightly to study him. Eyes white and hollow, the only visible part in the void of blackness that lay before him. Terror surged through Mel's body, draining him of energy, making it harder and harder to breathe. But still he stood, rooted to the spot.

Only one thought ran through his mind, over and over again. *Remember the Stone. Remember the Stone.* Where was Ĵan? Had he begun his attack? Had the Stone done nothing at all? Maybe it hadn't worked…

The doubt weakened him further. No. He couldn't afford those thoughts.

The hands closed over Mel's body and dragged him forward. Their coldness blistered his skin, burned through the sleeves of his shirt, and he cried out in pain. The sound was swallowed in the oblivion.

And then it was completely silent. The world was gone, all sight and sound drained away, so that he hung suspended in a cloud of blackness. Frozen in another world. Silent.

Except for the voice.

What an interesting mortal. He has nearly beaten you. You were tricked.

The Darkness hissed in the distance.

Someone was speaking, a voice Mel didn't recognize.

He tricked you, you foolish wraith. Even when Caer Sia was within your grasp. Ah well. Your death will pave the way for us, in the same way that the Jewel did. It will open the gates.

Mel opened his eyes a crack, his mind foggy with pain. It was pitch black. The cold hands no longer gripped him, nor did he feel anything beneath him. He floated in a void. *I'm dead,* he thought vaguely. And yet… he still felt the cold hilt of his dagger, as well as the stinging, frost-bitten burns that seared his arms where the wraith had gripped him.

Stand down, Darkness. You've lost, as you can see. Now is the hour of us. Now is the hour of your master.

A flash of blue fire, barely a pinprick of light, appeared from far away. Mel saw it flashing, flickering, striking against the shadows that enveloped his vision. He heard another hiss from above, frustrated, admitting defeat.

Wise choice. Now let me see the boy.

A smooth cold hand cupped his chin and lifted his head, and now the unfamiliar voice that had spoken to the Darkness filled his mind. Agony flared behind his eyes and he cried out.

Ah, so much determination. Bravery, yes. Foolishness too—those are never a good mix, I might add. Ah, but there is so much more to you than meets the eye… how interesting…

"Who are you?" Mel managed to croak. His voice echoed and faded into the black oblivion around him. Still he saw nothing of the speaker. Then, slowly, a shape swam into form directly in front of him.

A face. Night gray skin, skull-like features chiseled as if carved from black marble, the eyes purple-red…

Very interesting. Are you sure you want to play this game, boy? You can still walk away… no? I sense your desires. You still want to help, to fight. Ah, and there is something else in you still, something I can use… it is your fear, child.

"Who…" Mel started again—the pain flared again, and he choked on the words—there was another flash of blue light, and this time he could see fire reflecting on a blade that had plunged through the Darkness' shadowy form… he heard a final, dying hiss as the wraith surrendered…

His vision focused on the face once more. Wreathed in shadow, darker than the blackness around him. A ruler of another realm. And the face smiled.

Thank you, boy. You have given me much interesting information. We shall be seeing each other very soon, I think.

Cold and darkness closed around Mel like water, holding him suspended, the icy chill of its touch seeping into his core.

The voice faded away, the last sentence repeating softly in Mel's mind.

We shall see each other soon.

Then came a final flash of blue fire, and in that moment, Mel's vision went out.

21

∽ ∽ ∽ ∽ ∽ ∽ ∽ ∽ ∽

Another Shadow

"Wake up, Mel, it's time for breakfast."

"Is he alive?"

"Come on son, you'll be late to studies…"

"Mel? Mel, can you hear me?"

"Time to wake up…"

Voices and memories swam through his mind, blending into a half-conscious, uncertain medley until he could no longer decipher which were real or not. He lay in the grass of his front yard. Misty was probably playing by the front door, giving him time to relax. His arms hurt… they stung. He must have stayed out in the sun for too long—he should have found some shade. But when the Darkness had killed him, he hadn't really—

Wait! When the Darkness had killed him? That wasn't right, because the pounding of his heart and the ache of his ragged lungs told him that he was—still very much alive.

He squinted and forced his eyelids open. Light blared in his vision, bringing with it a horrific headache. But the pain reinforced the startling realization that he was alive.

Two faces peered down at him, both surprised and concerned and, as he squinted up at them, very relieved. "Mel, can you move at

219

all?" The voice, though hoarse with weariness and filled with worry, was a familiar and trusted voice. Mel's vision blurred for another moment before focusing on Dandio's face.

Mel wiggled his arms and legs, or tried to, at least. The movements sent more pain from his aching muscles. But he could feel all his limbs. Everything still seemed intact, even if his whole body felt like it had been crushed in a vice. "Dandio?" he croaked, his voice weak.

The Liznee's weather-beaten face softened with a wide smile of relief. He looked so happy that Mel smiled too. The skin of his face felt tight and sore, as if it had forgotten the expression. "What happened?" he managed to rasp.

Jan knelt above him also. "You stopped the Darkness," the king said simply, smiling. "I admit I'm not sure how—we saw it grab you, and then you disappeared into the fog."

"Drisilas..."

"The stone stopped it," Dandio said. "Or at least, weakened it. But whatever you did first—it gave up. It withered away entirely." He straightened and let out a long breath. There was a look in both of the Liznee brothers' eyes—a deep satisfaction—and Mel realized how much this meant to them. At last, after all these years, their mother and many of their friends had been avenged. The Darkness had been destroyed.

Dandio took his arm and helped him stand. Every one of Mel's muscles felt shaky and uncertain, and he took a few wobbly steps. The ground around them was bare and charred, damp with melting ice. He looked up, back towards the castle. The last light of evening shone on Caer Sia. The city had survived to stand another day.

We'll see each other soon.

Mel looked up. "Wait—did you see anyone else? The Darkness—did it speak?"

Jan shook his head. "No. It hissed a few times when we attacked it. We could hear you calling something, and knew you were alive in there."

That didn't make sense... he had heard a voice. He knew he had. And he had seen that face...

Chills ran down his spine, and he stumbled. Dandio caught him and led him gently forward. "Come on. You are exhausted, and not surprisingly."

They moved toward the castle. Mel could see two figures standing by the doorway, peering anxiously out across the battle field. Rygal and Allie. Allie sprang down the steps and ran towards them, relief and joy on her face.

"Mel, are you all right?"

"Yeah..." Mel mumbled, feeling himself blush.

"You beat it—is it gone? What happened?" Allie demanded eagerly.

"It's gone," Dandio said with a slight smile as she hugged him in relief. "Now let Mel rest before you bombard him with questions. And let's talk about your own decisions," he added with a raised eyebrow. "I saw you join the battle—a battle I had specifically stated you stay out of."

Allie's face fell. But then a slight smile spread over her father's face, and he put an arm over her shoulders. "I'm very proud of you,

Asescia. You did very well. We'll work on your swordplay, though," he added. "It could use some improving."

Allie folded her arms indignantly as they entered the courtyard. "Really? Rygal said I did pretty good."

Dandio turned a withering look on the young warrior, who was grinning. "Did he," Dandio said, eying Rygal carefully. But he couldn't stop the smile from breaking through. "Very well. Come inside. Rygal, you need to have the doctors look at your injury too."

They made their way inside the castle. Three kragons flew to land in the courtyard, accompanying their massive lord. Mel couldn't help staring at them. Close up, the beasts were even more impressive. Their talons were streaked with blood. Adderstrike was gone. Jan paused to speak briefly to Lord Fireclaw and thank him for his timely assistance.

Dandio helped Rygal inside the palace, where two medics immediately took him away to the hospital rooms. Another doctor took Mel to the same area to treat the burns on his arms. Mel's head still ached and he felt too tired to do anything more than answer the occasional question the doctor asked him.

He had just been settled in bed when a small figure appeared in the doorway of the hospital. "Mel!" Misty sprang forward, climbing onto the bed and hugging her brother.

"Hey, Misty," Mel said with a grin.

"Are you okay? What happened?" Misty demanded. "Did we win?"

"We won," Mel told her, and felt his smile widen as the reality set in. "We won."

"Glad to hear it," came a familiar voice from the bed to his right. Dusty sat up, her injured leg stretched out in front her, the wound bandaged neatly.

"You should have seen him, Dusty," Rygal said with a weak grin from the bed on Mel's other side. "He charged right in at the Darkness and gave Jan the time to strike it down. The Stone in Drisilas—that was the way to kill it."

Except the Stone hadn't really killed the Darkness… it had been ordered to back down. Ordered by a voice and an unknown face…

Mel's smile vanished as the thought filled his mind again. Rygal noticed, and frowned slightly.

"You all right, Mel? I'm just teasing you—you did great." Rygal winced as the doctors began probing his side, checking for broken bones.

"Yeah, I'm fine," Mel said vaguely, laying down as the doctor moved away from him. He felt too tired to think through all that had happened.

He heard Allie enter, speak to Dusty, and ask how they were all doing. The doctors informed Rygal that he had two broken ribs, and would need to stay in the hospital while they treated him.

"How'd you do that?" Dusty asked him critically.

"Adderstrike—did you see how far I flew in the air when he hit me? When Adderstrike's tail—" Rygal sounded pleased with himself.

"No, I didn't see it. I was on the battlement with Glentree."

"I saw," Allie said helpfully. "He probably flew twelve feet in the air and crashed into the wall."

"Hmm, that I would have like to see," Dusty said with a soft laugh.

Rygal sounded less-than-pleased. "It hurt," he mumbled.

The voices faded as Mel slipped into sleep. The doctors had applied a soothing balm and bandaged his arms, which cooled the burns. His head throbbed with the lingering headache, and the soft voice of the being within the shadows repeated over and over again in his thoughts.

The death of the Darkness will pave the way.

Just like the Jewel did.

Now is the hour of your master.

We'll see each other soon, I think.

In a haze of uncertain and exhausted dreams, he saw the face again, the purple-red eyes glittering as the face smiled, and the distant light from Drisilas shone on him—a withered, shapeless being, an ancient threat as old as the world, tattered ruin of fine robes draping the body, the face hollow and sunk like a skull in the pupil-less light of the eyes.

Mel jolted awake.

He guessed it was early morning by the light streaming in through the gap in the curtains on the far wall. The hospital was quiet, the injured still asleep. Rygal was snoring softly in the bed next to Mel's.

Mel got up stiffly. His body ached from the conflict yesterday, but he needed to talk to someone—tell them about the voice. Dandio would listen, he knew.

He didn't find Dandio, but Jan was speaking to Glentree in the hall outside the hospital rooms. "Oh—sorry, sire," Mel stammered quickly. "Where's Dandio?"

"Asleep, as should you be," Jan said with a half-smile. "Is there something I can help you with?"

"I just—I need to tell you something. About the Darkness," Mel said, gathering his thoughts. "When it grabbed me, I saw something else. I heard a voice, and—it told the Darkness to surrender. It told the Darkness to give up."

Jan frowned slightly. Glentree looked between Mel and the king. "It wasn't the Darkness' voice?" the giant asked Mel uncertainly.

"No, and it wasn't really coming from the Darkness, either. I mean—it felt like I was *inside* the place that the Darkness came from." Now they were looking at him like he was crazy. Mel pressed on determinedly. "I couldn't see anything, just blackness. And there was a voice that I didn't recognize talking to the Darkness, telling it that it had lost. But it said that the Darkness' death would… pave the way, like the Jewel did. It said it was the hour of its master."

The words meant nothing to Mel, only more confusing things that added to the confusion and terror of yesterday's battle. But the color had drained from Jan's face. "The hour of its master?" he repeated slowly.

"Yeah, what does that mean?" Mel demanded instantly.

Jan looked at Glentree, who looked uncertain. "Send for the scribes. I must send a message to Iriam."

Glentree nodded and jogged away down the hall.

Mel looked up at the king, in an agony of unknowing. "Sire, what is it? What's going on?" A chill ran through him. "I'm not—possessed, am I?" He remembered how the Darkness had controlled the serpentines and spoken through them. Had it done something to him?

"No, you are not," the king reassured him. "And you may call me Ĵan. This city—no, all of Coonsia—owes you a great debt. You helped stop the Darkness, and for that I am very grateful. But some things… some things are better left unexplained for now."

"That's what Dandio said about the Darkness, and then it ended up being pretty important," Mel said bluntly. He realized how rude that sounded, but he was tired of adults pretending he was too young to understand. Sure, he was only eleven, but he had just helped defeat the Darkness. Had almost died doing it. At least they could tell him what was going on.

Ĵan looked at him and shook his head slowly. "Mel, I am not slighting you this information. I don't know what is going on yet, not without council." His green eyes scanned the hall, then he turned to Mel. "Come with me." They walked down the corridor, past a few groups of talking courtiers, and down a short flight of stairs.

Mel followed the tall Liznee inside a candle-lit room that smelled of ink and books. A desk with a tea set was placed in the corner, next to a window that looked north over the sea. Books and papers were stacked neatly on top of it. Two wooden chairs sat near the desk.

"Sit," Ĵan told him. Mel did so, practically bursting with questions. The king sat across from him behind the desk. "Would you like tea?"

Mel nodded slightly but stayed on focus. "Sire—Jan—who do you think the voice was?"

Jan poured him a cup of tea. "Tell me. Tell me everything you heard the voice say."

Mel told him all of it, as many details he could remember. The last sentence had chilled him the most, the one that continued to echo in his mind. But the only part that Jan reacted to was the news before that. *"There is something in you I can use—your fear, child."* That part hadn't made much sense to Mel, but the king only nodded thoughtfully.

"Who do you think it was?" Mel asked as soon as he had finished recounting it all.

Jan thought for a moment. "How much do you know about the realm the Darkness came from?" he asked.

Mel frowned, thinking. When Dandio had first explained the Darkness, there hadn't been much information about the wraith's homeland. "Not much," he admitted. "I think Dandio told us… that it came from the same place that the Netrocrians did. But I don't know much about them at all."

"Well, not many of us do," Jan said. He paused. "I will tell you what we know, if only to ease your mind," he said finally. "But you must understand, this is a very difficult subject. We know dangerously little about these other powers—though in the past few years, they have reintroduced themselves, and we have learned more."

"What other powers?" Mel asked.

"Did Rygal tell you about the Jewel of Power?" Jan asked. Mel nodded—Rygal had told them several stories about the quest two years before. "The Jewel was thought to be no more than a weapon," Ĵan explained. "A dangerous weapon, yes, but useless unless someone wielded it."

"Like Drisilas," Mel said slowly.

Ĵan nodded. "Well, the two are related, it seems. The Star-Stone in Drisilas' hilt came from the Land Immortal. The realm beyond life, a resting place for all that is pure. The kingdom of the High Light."

"And the Jewel did, too?" Mel guessed.

"So we assumed. After all, all Safacon explained of it was that the Jewel was created from the core of a dying star. But when Norrin—he was the leader on the quest for the Jewel—sent us his report, he said that the Jewel was more than what we had believed. It was called a doorway, uncontrolled, unrestrained. If its power had successfully enveloped Gayrile, I doubt we would be here now."

Mel took a sip of his tea, not sure what to say. The voice from the dark void filled his mind again and another fact resurfaced. "Wait—that's what the voice said, too. It said that the Darkness' death would pave the way for them to come. Like the Jewel did."

The Liznee king nodded again, looking thoughtful. "Mel, just as the Star people were once the guardians of all that is pure in the world, there is another place—another ruler—for everything that is dark. Light is stronger than darkness, but until all is made whole at the end of time, there will always be a certain power associated with evil. The rebel Netrocrians sought this power centuries ago, until desire practically drove their leader mad."

"Their leader? Was that—the Darkness?"

"No, the Darkness was only one of his creations." Ĵan hesitated. "As I said, we know very little about this ruler. That's one thing I hope to learn from Iriam the Neutral—he alone may have some clue of what we are up against. For now, I can tell you this." He leaned forward, hands clasped together on the desk. "There is a power beyond our world, one who has been orchestrating everything that has happened in the last few years. Kado and the Hazes, the Jewel, the Darkness reawakening—do you think this is all a coincidence?"

Mel shook his head slowly. "Who is it?" he asked in barely a whisper.

Ĵan hesitated again—Mel guessed he was trying to decide how much to tell. "We don't know," the king admitted. "But if you want my personal opinion, it is the same leader of darkness who brought about the Dividing War. His name was Kahlifis—a Netrocrian with great power. Some believe he had the power to speak with the dead, to see the future. He was thought to be killed in the Dividing War."

"The Dividing War... but that was hundreds of years ago. Even if he escaped the battle, he'd be dead by now," Mel said, then added uneasily, "right?"

"Well, that is the question," Ĵan said, leaning back in his seat. "I don't want you to worry yourself with these matters, Mel. Whatever comes next, our fear will only be used against us."

Mel could hear the voice's message speaking in his head, sending chills down his spine. Ĵan was right. It wasn't a coincidence that the

Darkness had suddenly reawakened, two years after the Jewel of Power had been destroyed. It wasn't a coincidence that Llyrion had been killed, but none of the others.

And he knew, deep down, that the Darkness hadn't returned just because of Drisilas. It had been stirring before the sword was even stolen. Summoned by an unknown power. Someone was behind it all, he knew.

Perhaps it wouldn't be long before they found out who.

"It'll be here soon," Mel said out loud, taking a deep breath. "Jan… it said it'll be here soon. Kado and Safacon are out of its way. The Jewel has been destroyed, and the Darkness failed it. But next time… next time, I don't think it'll allow for failure. It's coming."

22

Mel's Purpose

They spent the next two nights in Caer Sia. Mel was eager to go home, but he knew that in the aftermath and confusion of the battle, it would be a little while longer for the Liznees to take them home. So much had to be done, and many of the roads heading east had been barricaded or damaged by Terrax.

At least the delay allowed the companions a little while longer to talk together. Dandio, Mel, and Misty gathered in the hospital room to visit their two injured comrades. Rygal was still recovering, and it hurt for him to move much. Dusty was also healing, and Mel could tell she was anxious to be on her feet again. The long gash on her leg would take weeks to heal fully, which had her in an irritable mood.

"The Wildkids need to hear of this," she said one evening as they gathered in the hospital again. She sounded frustrated. "The Darkness' destruction will bring about much, especially in the east. And I doubt we've seen the last of Terrax."

"You're leaving then?" Mel asked her.

"As soon as my leg is better," Dusty said. "It's good that the Darkness was destroyed, but in truth, fear of it kept many of the N'Tell's enemies at bay. I assume they will begin to stir again, once they hear that it's gone."

Misty's face fell. "Then we might not see you again."

Dusty smiled gently at her. "Maybe not for a little while. There's much to be done. But I will write to you, if you wish."

Misty looked up hopefully. "Yes, I'd like that. I've never had a pen-pal before. I can't wait to tell Mama!" She looked so excited at this idea that it made the others chuckle softly.

Mel had more questions. "What about Terrax, Dandio?" he asked slowly. "He escaped. Do you think he'll try to…" he trailed off, leaving the awful question unasked.

"Try to take down Caer Sia again?" Dandio finished for him, and Mel nodded. The tall Liznee thought for a moment. "I doubt Terrax will ever give up his mission. He is determined to prove himself the heir of the Elven people, and to form his own sort of kingdom. But to answer your question, Mel, I think Coonsia is safe from him. With Drisilas safely within Sia's walls again, he will have to search elsewhere for his source of power. No, Terrax's goal lies elsewhere, and the Red Dawn will continue to hunt for him. He has vanished into the woods near Elimar now."

"Then do we ride to Elimar?" Rygal asked immediately, sitting up. He winced as the movement jolted his injured ribs.

"Not now," Dandio said with a faint smile. "For now, rest assured that I will tell you when you are needed. All of you," he added, as Mel started to ask another question.

And Mel knew that would be all for now. Like Dandio had said multiple times before, it didn't do any good to worry about things before they happened.

He and Misty returned to the room they had been staying in, across the hall from the hospital room. He tucked Misty into bed; she looked up at him with wide, worried eyes.

"What's wrong?" Mel asked.

Misty hugged the blankets to her chin. "I'm scared, Mel," she confessed. "What if the bad creatures come back?"

"Don't worry," Mel reassured her. "We're going home soon. The Darkness is gone. We're safe."

"Are we?" Misty asked softly. Her brow was furrowed, her eyes wide and fearful.

Mel paused. "Yeah," he said shortly, but the question lingered in his mind as he lay down in the bed across from hers. Danger had always been in this world, he knew… yet now, oddly enough, his senses felt tuned to it. He found himself waking at any faint noise in the hallway, his hand instinctively going to his hip where he usually kept his knife on him.

This quest, experiencing battle, seeing people die—that had done something to him. And he wasn't sure what.

He looked over at Misty, who was sound asleep. She was young enough, and she hadn't experienced the same things Mel had. It wouldn't affect her in the same way. She'd have a few hard months, and then most of her fear would fade.

But Mel… he knew he wouldn't just forget all this.

Even as he closed his eyes, the recent terror of the battle filled him. He saw Adderstrike snarling over Rygal, Terrax's sword slitting Drona's throat, the horrible white eyes as the Darkness bent over him.

And the hollow voice from the void beyond, echoing in his thoughts, haunting his dreams yet again.

He awoke to someone knocking lightly on the door.

"We're awake," he said, taking a breath. Misty sat up, her hair disheveled. Judging by the light outside, they had slept well—it appeared to be midmorning.

Allie appeared in the doorway. "Sorry to wake you up. Your carriage home will leave this afternoon, and my father and Ĵan want to speak with you two before."

Mel nodded. "All right—thanks."

The princess smiled and left.

Mel scooped Misty up out of bed, swinging her to the floor and making her giggle. He could tell some of her anxiety from last night had gone away with sleep. Now her face was lit with a big smile. "Are we going to go home?" she asked eagerly.

"I think so," Mel said. That thought drove away some of his dark thoughts, and he felt himself smile too.

After getting dressed and eating breakfast, they met Ĵan and Dandio in the council hall. It was quieter now, with most people busy outside cleaning up the aftermath of battle.

"I know I speak for the whole city in saying thank you," Ĵan told them. "What you two did was remarkable, saying nothing of your youth or experience. Dandio has told me what you did on the quest as well, and it sounds like you were both very brave."

Mel and Misty exchanged glances, both of them pleased by the praise but not sure what to say. "Well… we don't feel like we did much, sire," Mel admitted finally. It didn't seem right to accept the praise without some confessions. "We got in the way, we had to be rescued an awful lot—Dandio almost died saving my life." He looked at the tall Liznee warrior.

"Humility is a good trait in any warrior," Dandio said thoughtfully. "And I don't measure bravery by how much you fight. What I saw were two children, both a little scared, both a little excited, who obeyed orders and didn't complain even on long days of walking. That, I have to say, is more than can be said for many of my soldiers."

Mel looked up at his hero, a warm satisfaction filling him at the praise. That and the fact that Dandio Ki was proud of him.

Misty looked up at Ĵan. "Sire—could we please go home?"

Ĵan smiled at her and nodded. "Yes, Misty. We will send you on our fastest carriage east, and arrange for a resting place along the way—you will likely arrive home by tomorrow morning."

Home. They were going home. "Thank you, sire," Mel said, smiling as he thought of it.

They went to say good bye to their companions—Glentree was busy with the army and Dusty, despite her injury, was preparing to sail to the far east again. Misty asked her a heap of questions about the Wildkid's home, which Dusty answered patiently and willingly while Mel talked with Rygal.

"Are you going back to Gayrile?" he asked.

"Probably in the next few days. I've been going back and forth between Caer Sia and Gayrile over the last two years, after Safacon was defeated," Rygal told him. "Reporting to Dandio and so forth."

"Right," Mel said. Suddenly, the thought of returning to Appledale wasn't that important. Now he realized what he would leave behind. This world of adventure and bravery and danger—danger aplenty, of course, but that didn't matter as much anymore, not when he knew he was facing the danger to help someone. Leaving this world of heroism that he had once only dreamed of. Now he had gotten the chance to experience it, to live in it, to embark on this quest. And now it felt strange to leave it behind and return to normal life.

His expression must have changed, because Rygal frowned. "Everything all right?"

"Yeah," Mel said, not sure how to put it into words. "It's just… I feel different now. This quest—for the first half of it, I just felt in the way. But then everything happened, all the dangerous stuff that I didn't think I'd ever be able to face—but I realized I could. And we were able to save Caer Sia, and save a lot of people from the Darkness—it sounds weird, but I feel like that's where I belong."

Rygal nodded thoughtfully. "I understand exactly, Mel. That's how I felt after we stopped Kado. Like I wanted to do something, but I didn't know what."

"I guess… I just don't want this to go away," Mel said, gesturing vaguely. Then an idea came to him. "Misty—can I have a piece of paper?"

Misty, halfway through carefully writing out their address to give to Dusty, passed him a page and a pencil. Mel wrote quickly and much less carefully. "This is our address—will you write to me if anything happens?" He paused, realizing what he was asking. "I mean, I'm not saying I have to be invited on another quest or anything, just—the only information we get in Appledale is month-old rumors."

Rygal took the page and grinned. "Sure, Mel. I'll let you know. Might be sooner than you think."

Mel frowned slightly at his words. "I'm not sure I'll… be back," he said slowly. Knowing his mom, the moment he and Misty got home, they would be kept in the safety of their house for months before she let them go anywhere again.

Rygal thought for a moment. "Neither was I," he said, giving him that crooked grin again.

And those words lingered in Mel's mind as he and Misty made their way down the halls to the courtyard. A carriage had been prepared to take them home. Dandio stood beside it, waiting for them.

"Have a safe ride back," the Liznee said as he lifted Misty inside. He turned to Mel. "I don't think I ever properly thanked you for bringing us the sword in the first place, Mel."

Mel shrugged slightly. He was running out of things to say in response to thank you. "I'm glad I could help," he said.

Dandio took his shoulders and looked him straight in the eyes. "Remember what you did here, Mel. Remember what you are capable of, and never forget it."

Mel felt his face warm at the praise. "I'm not sure I'll ever be able to do something like that again," he admitted with a rueful smile.

What had happened in the battle—his actions had felt almost instinctive. He had acted because if he hadn't, someone would have died instead.

Dandio studied him, that familiar half-smile playing on his features. "You will," he said simply. "When the time comes… I think you will."

He helped Mel up into the carriage. Mel stared at Dandio as he sat down, not understanding what the words meant. Rygal and Dandio had both hinted at something today. Like they knew something he didn't. Something Jan had only mentioned.

His mind felt full with thoughts as the carriage started off. Misty watched the city and the terrain speed by as they headed east, then finally dozed off, fast asleep in her seat. Mel studied her, thinking. It wasn't any problem for her. She was perfectly happy to return home to Appledale. To safety and school and their family.

Mel wasn't sure why he didn't feel the same. Yes, he couldn't wait to see his family again, to tell them about all they had been through. But he didn't like the idea that things would go back to the way they had been, before he had ever heard of serpentines and flaming swords and the Darkness.

Somewhere, deep in his soul, he could feel a tug, a call back to action. He wasn't sure when it had started. Perhaps it had flickered to life at the low challenge of the voice within the blackness, a voice that even Jan hesitated to speculate on. But somehow, Mel knew he would return to the fight.

But when? Why? What circumstances could ever prompt him

to return and witness the carnage and the blood and the pain? To watch a companion die without being able to do anything? That grief—that fear—it would stay with him for the rest of his life.

Rygal's words echoed in his mind. Had he sensed the conflict in Mel? Or…or did he know something Mel didn't?

Mel remembered Dandio's fearless actions as he fought the serpentine, or Llyrion, fighting Terrax's outlaws. Mel wanted to be like them. He didn't want to be rescued—he wanted to save lives.

He wanted to be a hero.

He figured it was a childish notion. Would he seriously return to Caer Sia, return to the madness and the tangle of war when it arose?

Somehow, he guessed that he would.

Epilogue

My dear friend Iriam,

I trust this message finds you in good health. It is sent, I fear, with the utmost urgency. You have likely heard of the circumstances that have brought about the destruction of the Darkness. Drisilas has been safely returned, thanks to the efforts of a few courageous companions. The traitor Pellion Drona has been killed, while his counterpart Terrax remains at large.

Yet these are not the reasons I write to you. With the Darkness' destruction comes many questions. We were grateful to have the help of a brave young boy named Mel, from Appledale. In the last moments of the battle, he experienced the Darkness' power up close, before its destruction. In that moment, a voice spoke to him, a voice beyond the shadows. This voice did not come from the Darkness; instead, it ordered the wraith to stand down. There is much information that Mel explained, but the most important part of it is this:

Now is the hour of the Darkness' master.

My friend, I only have theories of who this voice might belong to, and the very idea of it, I admit, is chilling to comprehend. Strange times are coming, and the master of dark has invited us to a dangerous game. Yet the time will come to face him. I have no doubt that he will come, eventually.

I have already sent messages to many of our other allies. Norrin of Gayrile will hear of this, as will King Casper of the Direns. I hope to receive your advice speedily. You alone may have some idea of how to best defeat what lies ahead.

I remain, servant of the Light,

Ĵan Ki

To be continued…

Glossary/Pronunciation Guide

Adderstrike (AH-der-strike)
rogue kragon with a grudge against the Liznees

Ajaha Ki (ah-ZHA-ha KEE)
Dandio's wife; a skilled courier

Appledale
a small town in Daffodalion

Asescia Ki (ah-SESS-see-ah KEE)
daughter of Dandio and Ajaha; heiress to the crown of Caer Sia

Caer Sia (care SEE-uh)
the capital of Coonsia; home of the Liznees

Cantrians (CAN-tree-ins)
most common type of Essence-filled being; includes humans and elves

Coonsia (COON-see-uh)
a country in the northern Mainland of Orlell

Daffodalion (DAFF-oh-DAHL-lee-in)
Coonsia's neighbor; the largest country on the Mainland

Dandio Ki (dan-DYE-oh KEE)
commander of Caer Sian army, brother of the High King

Drisilas (DRISS-ah-lass)
a flaming sword of power, owned by the High King

Dusty
fiery and skilled Wildkid warrior

Dwarves
a race of stocky warriors native to Daffodalion

Fireclaw
the king of the kragons; ally to the Liznees

Fyrocrians (FY-roh-CREE-ins)
a type of Essence-filled being whose power manifests as fire and light

Glentree
Dandio's second-in-command

Jan Ki (ZHAN KEE)
High King of the Liznees

Kalos-Lia (KAY-lohs LEE-uh)
Hama-dryad archer

Kasabren (KASS-ah-bren)
a distant island country; home of the Wildkids

Kragons (KRA-guns)
large and intelligent winged creatures native to Coonsia

Liznees (LIZ-nees)
a race of silver-skinned Fyrocrians native to Coonsia

Llyrion Tarash (LEER-ee-on tah-RASH)
elven captain in the Red Dawn

Mel Smallbutton
a young boy from Appledale

Misty Smallbutton
Mel's little sister

Munben-Lia (MOON-bin LEE-uh)
leader of the tribe of Lia; Kalos' grandfather

Nella
Dandio's trained gryphon

Pellion Drona (PELL-ee-on DROH-nuh)
steward of Caer Sia

The Red Dawn
a sect of elite warriors that serve Caer Sia

Rygal (RYE-gull)
young warrior and member of the Guardians of Gayrile

Serpentines (SER-pen-TEENS)
snake-like creatures that serve an unknown master

Tackert Fief
a tiny village southwest of Appledale

Terrax (TERR-axe)
an elven outlaw

Acknowledgements

Once again, thank you to my family for your ongoing love and support as *The Orlell Chronicles* takes flight into publication.

My mom Leslie has once again offered her invaluable skills as an editor. Thanks for all the misspelled words, the grammatical errors, and the plotholes that you caught in each draft of book 3.

I also want to thank my dear in-laws. Not many people are willing to listen to the over-energized rambles of a fantasy writer. Your genuine interest and excitement for the story means so much to me, and I love all the inside jokes I can share with you both. (The elves make the shoes).

Thank you to the Writer's Group of Calvary McMinnville, for reading the early drafts of the first 3 chapters and giving such great feedback as the story was set up. Your encouragement to me is so valued, and I love the community and passion for writing that we share.

To the many readers who, following the end of book 2, immediently began asking about its sequel. Your feedback and support means more than I can explain. I could not ask for a better fanbase.

And to my husband Levi. *The Quest for Drisilas* would not be the same without your help. Thanks for your advice, your hard questions, your edits, and your love.

All honor be to God!

www.ingramcontent.com/pod-product-compliance
Lightning Source LLC
Chambersburg PA
CBHW011240200726
48288CB00018B/3403